Jack Hammond is a Native of Scipio, Indiana. While growing up, he was active in sports, participating in wrestling, football and track. Upon completion of high school, Jack initially attended Jamestown College North Dakota on a wrestling scholarship. After completion of his first semester, he transferred to Vincennes University, earning his Associate in Applied Science. In 2006 Jack Hammond enlisted in the United States Army where he has now served for 15 years. Throughout his service, Jack has been deployed once to Iraq and two times to Afghanistan. He is married to Jerri Hammond and they have four children.

Thank you for taking time out of your Schedule to take a look at my Novel if you could please do a review on it, it would be greatly Appreciated

First Sergeant
Jack Hammond
U.S. Army

To my wife, and father:

Once again you have encouraged me to continue to pursue my dreams. It is because of you two that publishing has become possible. Without your encouragement, I would not have been able to achieve this milestone.

Jack Hammond

ECLIPSE 8

AUSTIN MACAULEY PUBLISHERS™

LONDON • CAMBRIDGE • NEW YORK • SHARJAH

Ordering Information
Quantity sales: Special discounts are available on quantity purchases by corporations, associations, and others. For details, contact the publisher at the address below.

Publisher's Cataloging-in-Publication data
Hammond, Jack
Eclipse 8

ISBN 9781685624460 (Paperback)
ISBN 9781685624477 (ePub e-book)

Library of Congress Control Number: 2023906022

www.austinmacauley.com/us

First Published 2023
Austin Macauley Publishers LLC
40 Wall Street 33rd Floor, Suite 3302
New York, NY 10005
USA

mail-usa@austinmacauley.com
+1 (646) 5125767

Chapter 1
The Interview

As the president of the Lunar Intergalactic Higher Transportation Agency or L.I.G.H.T. Agency entered the dome shaped building with a sign that read "Space Exploration," he could feel his anticipation grow. He knew that he would be asked many questions he did not want to answer or could not answer. Now inside the building he made his way to front of the large auditorium to a dimly lit stage to talk to the space exploration contributors, enthusiasts, and citizens that had gathered to hear of the agency's newest endeavors. Once in front of the microphone, he began by saying, "Space holds limitless possibilities! There are many areas that we conduct studies in, that we have barely began to scratch the surface of. Areas that could lead to discoveries that would change humanity as we know it. Recent research has led us to believe that the future of space exploration lays in the study of black holes. That being stated, we are looking into this research and preparing to act, as we are composing a plan to send one of our state-of-the-art ships into the black hole we have named Nexus 12, to gather information and conduct research. It is our hope that we are able to find new planets to inhabit. If we are unable to find new inhabitable planets, we are at least hoping to find resources that would better the current global state of affairs."

As soon as President Hays finished with his statement, the contributors silence was immediately broken. A room that had once been so quiet you could hear the particulates floating through the air was quickly filled with shouting. Trying to create order, President Hays said, "One at a time, please. I will answer all of your questions that time permits. However, I would like to keep some type of order so that each question receives a proper response. If you could, please raise your hand and wait to be called on. If I am unable to answer your questions today or I feel that I cannot answer the question that is asked with 100% certainty, I will write your question down and consult with my research team. Once we have found the answer to your question, I will then contact you and let you know the answer that has been concluded."

Upon finishing his statement, the first individual raised their hand quickly. Now having everyone's attention, the individual began speaking, "Through research that has been funded entirely by donations, which were generously given to you, primarily from those in this room. What knowledge have you been able to gain that you were unable to in the past? How is it that the billions of dollars spent in research, is just now leading you to believe that the answer to interstellar travel and survival lies in black holes? A void or theoretical mass that has existed and has been known about long before you or the L.I.G.H.T. agency?

"At this point, travel to other galaxies has proven to be very time consuming and has not yielded results that would warrant continued efforts. We have traveled to and beyond the Triangulum Galaxy, and have found no planets that could sustain human life. We have continued to be successful in finding resources. However, occupants of earth are continuing to consume those resources as quickly as we are able to recover them. As far as money spent on exploits, myself and the L.I.G.H.T agency are very gracious for you and your contributions. All money that is donated continues to go towards research, equipment, and operations, all of which are not cheap. Lastly, research on black holes is no new exploit. This research has been conducted long before I, or any of my staff came into existence. So, with that comment, you are correct. We have always known, or have been led to believe that black holes may be the key to interstellar travel. However, there has never been enough evidence to support this hypothesis. Due to recent research though, we believe that we are now in a position to attempt travel into Nexus 12 for the first time."

After President Hays finished with this comment, another individual immediately began speaking. "President Hays, why now, are you led to believe that this travel will be possible? Have you successfully sent anything into a black hole? And if you have, have you been able to retrieve any of those items?"

President Hays not wanting to answer the question, but knowing it would arise again, then replied, "L.I.G.H.T. has been able to send rovers and cameras into Nexus 12. When these items entered Nexus 12 in the past, they were able to send back photographs and data that helped pave the way for new studies. Some, but not all, of these items, have been able to be retrieved successfully. As with anything though, success is not always gained through accomplishments but many times through failure. If it doesn't work the first time, that doesn't mean you shouldn't do it again. Instead, you have simply found out what not to do. We do not have the exact science down yet, but the successful retrieval rate at this point is far higher than the loss rate. We do know, because of data gathered and tests that have been conducted, that black holes differ in types, and overall dynamics. Items placed in black holes with similar characteristics to Nexus 12 have a 70% retrieval rate. We are able to send items in, and retrieve them at the same point of entry. However, when testing was conducted on other black holes it was found that items may enter at one point or location and exit in a completely different location. That is if they reappear or are able to be retrieved at all."

As soon as president Hays finished with his comments, the next patron then asked, "You said that not all rovers and cameras have been successfully retrieved, how do you and your team of researchers plan on correcting or solving this problem? Or is there a solution?"

President Hays then replied, "Right now, I have researchers working around the clock conducting testing on the various black holes within our galaxy. These researchers are trying to find out which black holes have the highest retrieval rate for objects sent in. They are also working on a formula to alter these theoretical masses, so that we can ensure that items sent in return to the same point of entry."

Not missing a beat, the individual then responded, "What if your researchers' formula is wrong? What if you are never able to ensure that items, or more importantly individuals in this case, return to the same point of entry?

Because, let's face it, the science is not always exact, as you stated before. Are you able and willing to send these men and women to their fate?"

President Hays then responded, "If the worst should happen and our formula is wrong, then we will ensure that the crew of the ship are equipped with all of the supplies needed for survival."

"The ship that is under construction now is state-of-the-art and is unlike any that has been built previously or even dreamed of, it will be able to sustain life indefinitely. The blueprints for this ship include an atrium which will be fitted with fruit and vegetable producing plants, as well as, an irrigation system that will reuse water not absorbed by the plants. This will help to eliminate water waste. The plants will also help in reproduction of oxygen and discarding of carbon monoxide. We are also researching systems that will be able to collect particles floating in space that can be used. These systems would be placed on the exterior of the ship, and the particles collected would be directed to a part of the ship where scientists can separate them and put them to proper use. Also, as we hope that they are not needed, the ship will be fitted or equipped with weapon systems. Although we have not seen anything through research that indicates that there are lifeforms that would cause harm. We have put these systems in place so if faced with a life and death situation the crew would be able to defend themselves. Lastly, a platoon or small group of military personnel will man the ship. These individuals will be responsible for keeping good order on the ship and accompanying ground parties when conducting research on new planets. The name of the ship will be Eclipse 8, as it was the eight-design proposed. Before this mission takes place, there will be comprehensive testing conducted on all systems. If, during this planning process any problems are encountered that are not able to be overcome, then we will delay the mission until the problem can be resolved. In closing, does anyone have any other questions that have not been answered?"

After President Hays asked his final question, the room remained quiet for a minute. Then a retired Captain that once flew with President Hays asked, "Who will man this ship and who will captain it? Also, how will you train these individuals for an uncertain future? Even with adequate research there is always a possibility that the research is flawed or swayed to get the results that you want. In this case, if the worst was to happen, they would never get to return to their loved ones here and would be stuck on a ship that would prolong the inevitable, death. That in mind, will the individuals who man this ship be made aware that there is a possibility that they may never return?"

President Hays then answered, "When we signed up at this same Academy many years ago, we knew what we were signing up for. We knew that a situation may arise that required us to give our lives for the betterment of man. Sometimes we must sacrifice the lives of a few for the many. This situation is no different. All men and women manning the ship will be made aware of the possible dangers they may encounter before embarking on this mission. If any individual decides that they do not want to accept the risk associated with it, then we will find someone that is willing to take the risk."

After closing with this statement, President Hays exited the stage and made his way to a small ship that awaited him outside the building. Once aboard, he let out a sigh of relief. He was glad that the interview was over, but knew that there was a lot of work that still needed to be accomplished before the mission actually ensued. Several hours later, now aboard the Deep Space Station he made his way back to his quarters. Once in his quarters President Hays sat and reflected on the closing questions that his once comrade had made. Although all individuals that go through the Academy are made aware of the dangers that they may face, they rarely were. This time, however, President Hays felt that they would be faced with these dangers, and although he did not want this mission to take place, he had little choice. Contributors, commissioners, deep space committees, and presidents of almost every country informed him that this mission had to take place. Mankind had used almost all of the resources that were available to them in the galaxy that they inhabited and efforts to retrieve resources from nearby galaxies was proving to cost more than the results that were being yielded. If this mission didn't occur mankind may seek to exist.

Chapter 2
The Mission

Although President Hays told contributors that they had no reason to believe that other life forms existed and that the mission would simply be to conduct research and exploration, in hopes of finding new inhabitable planets and resources, that was not entirely true. The truth was that many variables and factors were being hidden from the media and contributors. The primary mission was research and exploration; however, there were some signs that other life forms did exist and were present. Whether they were peaceful or not was unknown. However, President Hays, as well as researchers, knew if these facts were revealed to contributors and the media it would bring their operations to a standstill. A standstill that could mean the extinction of mankind.

Some of the rovers that had been sent to conduct research and collect various types of samples from the planets within the black holes, ended up collecting more than was expected. Scientists and researchers were only hoping for possible pictures of inhabitable planets, resources that could replace or better substances already in use, or samples of soil that could be used for planting crops or nutrient replenishment. As most of the soil on Earth's surface had been depleted of its nutrients, and crops were being grown in genetically altered soil, that in turn made food taste bland. However, during one of the earlier rover missions they ended up collecting a microchip while soil samples were being gathered. The microchip at first looked like it was simply a metallic based rock fragment. However, when researchers looked at the sample closer, they could see the integrated circuits within it. When researchers discovered this, it led them to believe that it had probably been from other companies trying to conduct the same type of operations and research. However, there were no numbers or markings anywhere on the microchip that could link it to another company. Upon trying to hook the microchip up to test it and find out what its function was or what information could be recovered, it was found that the technology was way more advanced than any they had ever seen. All information gathered from the microchip came up in an unrecognizable language.

In later missions' photos that were taken revealed items that looked much like ships. Although, in many of the photos the objects were blurred due to the angle or speed of the camera taking the photo. It was because of this and other factors that no one person would verify that the object in question was a ship. Everyone felt that if they identified the blurred object as a ship, they would lose all credibility among their peers.

These photos did cause L.I.G.H.T., however, to create a secondary mission that was to be kept secret from everyone, except the crew and select individuals throughout the L.I.G.H.T. Agency. This secondary mission was to make contact with these ships. That is, if the objects in the photos were in fact ships. Once contact was made, they were to attempt to forge peace and trade treaties before other companies or agencies could beat them to it. If treaties were able to be forged and proved to be legitimate after the first sixty days, then the treaties would be handed to the L.I.G.H.T. Agency Board of Directors, who in turn would continue the operations.

The possible ships seen in the photos were also the real reason that Eclipse 8 was being fitted with weapon systems and military personnel. The military personnel were meant to assist in keeping order and accompanying ground parties as stated by the president. However, they were also going on the mission so that if a military crisis arose, someone trained in military tactics would be able to take charge when politics and negotiations failed. Whether they had to accomplish this by using the state-of-the-art weapon systems that the ship had been fitted with or by diffusing the situation through one sided negotiations.

Although President Hays had not talked about it in the interview, the ship was also fitted with another feature. This secondary feature was much like a shield. However, instead of simply stopping incoming fire, the added feature would allow the ship to absorb incoming fire or disintegrate it, depending on what was fired at the ship. If the incoming fire or blast was electrical the ship would turn the hostile fire into excess power that would be added to the charge fired by the ships weapon system. In turn, the electric charge fired from the ship would be supercharged. If the blast was not electrical it would break the incoming charge or round down into particles that would then be absorbed into the ships exterior system and rerouted to where it would be of the most benefit.

President Hays knew that L.I.G.H.T.'s secrets needed to be protected and remain secure at all costs. One of President Hays biggest concerns was that other individuals within the L.I.G.H.T. organization that were not part of the operation or did not agree with the operation would notice the modifications being made and start asking questions. Knowing that the modifications had not been cleared by the contributors that donated the money used for them, these individuals would then leak the information in hopes that they would receive a reward. As a safeguard to keep this from happening, President Hays felt that the ship would need to be constructed in an area that would keep others from noticing them. However, no one place within the Deep Space Station would be safe from observation.

It was because of this that President Hays decided that the ship's construction should occur within the Moon's Inner Tunnel Space Station. This station was used when L.I.G.H.T. initially started their space exploration missions. However, had been abandoned after the Deep Space Station was constructed. Not only would the ship be constructed in this location but it would launch from this location as well. Individuals that would be responsible for the construction of the ship would man the Moon's Inner Tunnel Space Station and remain there until after the mission was underway. After construction was complete, select individuals with the proper clearance would then be moved to the location where the ship's crew was being trained. So that they could go over the systems in depth with those that would be operating them.

President Hays knew that precautions would need to be taken to ensure that crew members did not leak information that could jeopardize the mission as well. He knew that all members of the L.I.G.H.T. Academy, whether they be researchers or astronauts, were not to speak of missions that they were taking part in. However, this had never stopped individuals in the past from leaking important information. To prevent this from happening President Hays came to the conclusion that once the crew was selected, researchers and the selected crew would need to be moved to somewhere that would limit their interaction with others. To accomplish this President Hays decided that personnel that were going to be involved with the mission would be transferred to Deep Lunar Space Station Bravo.

Deep Lunar Space Station Bravo was actually part of the Deep Space Station. However, it was a lower section of the space station that could be detached and used in case of emergency, or it could be used as a secondary life sustaining space station. The original theory behind this portion of the space station was that if over population occurred, this portion of the ship could be detached and built onto to form a new space station the same size as the Deep Space Station itself. Since this detachable portion of the ship could sustain life, individuals would not have to be transported back and forth to the main space station for every day needs.

Up to this point the detachable portion of the ship had never been needed. To avoid individuals becoming suspicious of this portion of the ship being detached, President Hays would have personnel go into the computer system and add personnel to the space station records. The additional personnel would justify President Hays detaching the portion of the ship. Once Deep Space Station Bravo was detached from the main space station personnel playing a role in the mission would be moved to the detachment. After all personnel were aboard the detachment, they would be made aware of all aspects of the mission. After hearing all of the details of the mission to include the secrets that were being kept personnel would then be given the opportunity to decline participation. However, if they declined to participate in the mission they would be debriefed and held in the Moons Inner Tunnel Space Station until after the mission was underway. This would ensure that they did not go back to the Academy, society, or the Deep Space Station itself and spread the information they had been made aware of to others.

Chapter 3
Help from the Unexpected

After reaching a conclusion on how to keep the mission specifics secret it was time to select individuals that would man the ship. However, the crew that would man Eclipse 8 would have to be much different than crews from previous missions. The crew that would man Eclipse 8 would have to be able to follow regulations and protocol; however, they would also have to be able to think outside the box and be good in crisis situations. The crew would have to be good at solving problems that could not be solved using conventional methods. As the crew would not have immediate access to L.I.G.H.T. or the Deep Space Station if something were to go wrong, and there was no way to know if communications would be able to be received through the black hole.

As with any ship the most important member of the crew would be the captain. It would also be the hardest position to fill, as the captain would have to hold the crew together and keep them calm in all situations. This individual would need to be one that could take ideas and information given by the crew into consideration before making a decision if higher command was unable to be reached. He would need to share his ideas with his crew and at the same time be able to take some criticism from those under his command. All of which sounds easy, but while training at the L.I.G.H.T. Academy all personnel training to take command of a ship are only taught to give commands and follow regulation. Individuals training to take command were not supposed to listen to reasoning or information from other members of the crew. Instead, they were supposed to do exactly what L.I.G.H.T. told them to do or follow regulation documented in the books they were trained from. If they were unable to reach the L.I.G.H.T. Agency or find the printed regulation, they were taught to abort their mission until they could once again establish communication with the L.I.G.H.T. Agency or returned to the Deep Space Station. Which in this case might not be possible if research was wrong and the crew could not pass through the black hole back to their original location.

With all of this in mind President Hays knew that he would need help selecting this individual. However, the one-person President Hays knew could help in selecting the best individual to fill the role was also one of the main individuals that opposed the mission. The individual that could help President Hays in selecting the perfect captain was none other than Captain Jacob Owen. The same man that questioned President Hays during the interview with contributors of the L.I.G.H.T. Agency.

Captain Jacob Owen the same man that was responsible for President Hays being alive. Earlier in their career Captain Jacob Owen was known as a wild man or a kamikaze captain. He would take any mission given to him. Captain Owens not only took these missions but would accomplish the tasks given to him regardless of what the consequences were. Captain Owens had traveled to six different galaxies and been in charge of four different ships before he was relieved of command for not following orders received from his higher command. The order that led to his relief was refusing to leave a fellow comrade. When his comrades ship was damaged and was falling lifelessly through space. Captain Owens knew that it was just a matter of time before the ship smashed into an asteroid, planet, or random space debris.

Captain Owens had all but the captain and First Lieutenant off of the Panther II when he received orders from L.I.G.H.T. to leave remaining personnel and abort the mission. L.I.G.H.T. felt that it was too dangerous in the asteroid belt where the ship had been damaged to continue the mission. They felt that if Captain Owens did not abort, they would lose another ship. However, Captain Owens cut communications and claimed that his radios and tele-command had went out and retrieved the two individuals anyway. The First Lieutenant aboard that ship at the time was President Owens. Once back at L.I.G.H.T. Command Captain Owens went in front of an unforgiving board and in turn was relieved for failing to follow protocol and the orders of his superiors. However, Captain Owens accepted his punishment without remorse as he had higher regard for human life than the orders of individuals that had not been placed in the same situation.

President Hays knew that to convince Captain Owens he would need to let him know everything that was taking place, even if it meant revealing the agendas and factors that had not been discussed in the press conference. President

Hays knew that Captain Owens had been in previous situations that were similar and would be able to assist him in finding an individual that could perform well when placed in a situation where the outcome was all but certain. President Hays knew that the man selected to captain the ship would have to have the same characteristics as Owens, and who better to pick that person than Owens himself.

After working the courage up and knowing that there was no one else to turn to, it was time to find Captain Owens. However, it would not be a hard search. President Hays knew that Captain Owens was normally able to be found in the Deep Space Station Bar. Captain Owens had spent most of his time there since his decommission. He had, in a sense, become known as the Space Station drunk. Although few men knew the reasoning that he was no longer a captain, or why he spent all of his time there.

When the time came, President Hays found Captain Owens exactly where he thought he would be. While walking into the bar Owens was easily spotted surrounded by empty beer bottles and shot glasses. From the looks of things, Owens had been at the bar since he had left the conference. As President Hays approached Owens, Owens spotted him in the bar mirror. No more than President Hays went to touch Owens on the shoulder, Owens grabbed an empty beer bottle from the bar, spun around, and swung at President Hays, missing. When he missed President Hays with the beer bottle his momentum took him all the way to the floor. However, Owens didn't get up. Instead, Owens laid passed out on the floor where he landed.

At this point President Hays had two cadets take Owens to his quarters. Once at President Hays quarters, he had the cadets lay the man on the couch in his living area. Hours later Owens awoke to President Hays sitting at a desk across the room from him. Instead of going after the man again though, he simply looked at President Hays and said, "How long have I been out Jack?" President Hays said,

"About six hours." After the exchange of words, the two men sat quietly enjoying the silence before indulging in conversation.

Owens ended up being the first man to break the silence by asking President Hays, "What do you want? Because I would not be here unless you needed something."

President Hays then responded, "I need your expertise and someone just like you."

Owens immediately responded, "What do you mean? I washed out because I wasn't right for the L.I.G.H.T. Academy or Agency."

President Hays then said, "You weren't right for the people who were in command before me and their agenda. I on the other hand need someone just like you."

Owens sat for a moment and then replied, "I am guessing that this has something to do with the mission that was discussed in the press conference."

President Hays sat for a long period before finally responding. "It does have to do with the very same mission. Although there was a lot of information that was not able to be disclosed in the conference."

Owens responded, "I knew there was more to this mission than met the eye. But what makes you think that I want any part of it?"

President Hays then said, "If you didn't want any part of the mission then why do you have so many questions?

It's obvious that you are concerned about the safety of all of the cadets or you wouldn't have reacted the way you did."

Owens responded, "Maybe I just don't feel right sending our young men and women to their death."

"Jacob you were the best captain to ever come through this academy. You were released from service for not doing what the books or superiors said, but doing what was right. You acted out of instinct and from the heart despite the consequences that you knew you would face. For this mission I need someone that can act in the same manner that you did. I need someone that can go above and beyond what regulation or superiors tell them to do but at the same time keeps the lives of their crew at the top of their priority list."

Owens then said, "I will help you but it is because I want to make sure individuals manning this ship have a fighting chance. If you stick the wrong person in charge of the ship and regulation goes out the window, they will need someone strong in charge of them. Someone that won't fold under pressure but instead will rise to the occasion. However, if you want me to help you, I am to be reinstated. I will resign as soon as the mission returns."

President Hays simply looked at the man and then said, "Consider it done! I will issue your reinstatement papers first thing this morning. As far as rank you will remain a captain. Your uniform is in the back spare bedroom in the closet. That is if it still fits you. I took it when they cleaned out your locker. I had a feeling at some point in time it would be needed again." Owens simply acknowledged President Hays and then slowly made his way to where his uniform had been stored.

Chapter 4
The Chief Mechanic

Upon receiving his reinstatement Captain Owens and President Hays began their search for the perfect crew. The two men agreed that they would start their search in an unconventional manner that had not been attempted before. Instead of selecting a captain first and then having the captain select his own crew, the crew would be hand-picked by the two men and the captain would be selected last. The men felt that this would be better because in many cases the chosen captain would simply pick their friends regardless of their capabilities. If they picked the crew though, the selection would be based on skills and not friendship. Which would better the crew's chance of survival if they were not able to return through the black hole.

The two men began their search by looking for a Chief mechanic for the ship. The mechanic that they chose, however, would need to be able to make an engine work regardless if he had parts at his disposal or not. Because if the ship was unable to return through the black hole they would eventually run out of spare parts and have to figure out how to keep the ship moving until the parts they needed could be retrieved or fabricated. Surprisingly this search did not start at the academy though. President Hays knew of a promising mechanic that was from Japan. At one-point President Hays had offered the young man a full scholarship to the academy. However, the young man turned President Hays down and told him that the curriculum was not challenging enough, and he did not believe that true success came from staying inside of set guidelines.

With the mission at hand President Hays felt that the man would change his mind though. Originally if the man would have attended the academy, he would have had to simply follow regulations. However, with this mission the man would be able to express himself, and at the same time might have to go outside of regulation to help continue operations. That in mind, President Hays and Captain Owens scheduled a flight and planned their visit to Japan.

Upon arriving in Japan, President Hays and Captain Owens made their way to a small town on the outside of Tokyo where the man they were in search of had once lived and conducted his business affairs. However, to both men's disbelief all that remained was an empty home with boarded up windows. It looked as if the home had been abandoned or vacated for some time. Not knowing how to respond President Hays looked at Captain Owens and said, "Well I guess this was a short-lived visit. We should return to the Deep Space Station and see what other candidates there are to choose from." Captain Owens however looked at President Hays and replied, "If this guy is as good as you say he is, he is the only candidate for the job. We shouldn't give up hope. All this visit did is show us where he isn't. I bet if we look around enough, he will turn up somewhere. Let's take the day to try and find him, and if we can't get any leads, we will pack it up." President Hays somewhat shaking his head then responded, "I hate to admit it, but I think you are right on this. But the question is where do we even start?" Now standing deep in thought Captain Owens said, "We talk to strangers, we ask anyone who may know him, or even people that work in places that he would frequently visit. I bet someone in a part store or electronic store knows him and where he could be."

Taking Captain Owens' advice the two men began walking around town and asking individuals if they knew the man and if so where he may be located. After several hours and countless miles covered the two men were finally successful in their search. While talking to an individual in a part store, they were told that Sun Tu could be located in a small warehouse on the opposite side of town. Hays and Owens hearing this immediately loaded into their small craft and made their way to the location that the man spoke of.

Once at the warehouse Captain Owens looked at President Hays and told him that he might be the best individual to talk to the man. Hearing this President Hays said, "Why is it that you should be the one that talks to him?" Not missing a beat Captain Owens replied, "First off, he knows who you are and he said no to you in the past. You are a great man and mean well, but it will take convincing from someone he doesn't know. It will take convincing from someone that is neutral. Someone who knows how to bend the rules." President Hays thinking about Captain Owens comment then replied, "Will he think you are neutral though? You are wearing a uniform now as well." Captain Owens now standing outside the craft replied, "I can make myself seem neutral even with the uniform. However, you are one of the main faces of L.I.G.H.T. and neutral coming from you still isn't neutral." Captain Owens then closed the door and made his way to the building. To President Hays surprise though Owens did not knock. Instead, he simply opened the door and walked straight inside.

Upon entering the building, Owens saw no one. The building looked and smelled just as he thought it would though. The smell of burnt jet fuel, oil, and metal filled the air. There were inventions and small engines like nothing he had ever seen before sitting around the warehouse. Some looked to be complete and others you could easily tell were works in progress, as they had parts laying all around them. Owens now having made his way around most of the warehouse and seeing what the man was capable of, stood in place wondering where he was. However, moments later his question was answered when he noticed a man watching him from the shadows.

After noticing the man, Captain Owens which was not even a little startled, began to approach him. Once he was within arm's reach he then extended his hand and said, "I am Captain Owens Sun." Sun laughed as he looked at the man. He then said, "I told your L.I.G.H.T. representatives "no" before. My answer is still the same."

Hearing this, Owens looked at Sun, and then ripped his L.I.G.H.T. pin off of his collar in one swift motion, and said, "There now I am no longer a member of L.I.G.H.T. Will you talk to me now?"

Sun now confused then said, "Just because you're not wearing the pin doesn't mean that you aren't L.I.G.H.T. It just means you are out of uniform now, and maybe even a little crazy. However, I will say that you are not like the ones that came before."

Owens simply responded, "L.I.G.H.T took my commission years ago for not following their rules and regulations, believe it or not. I just recently put this thing back on. However, now I am coming to you for the same thing that I was relieved for. I need an individual that is not only smart, but can operate in extreme conditions, and is able to get things done regardless of the circumstances. The question is, are you as good as they tell me you are?"

Sun then responded, "Will I have the opportunity to go outside regulation and incorporate some of my own ideas?"

Owens quickly replied, "We would expect you to follow some protocols. There is no way around that. Everyone has someone they answer to and certain rules they must follow regardless of where they work or what they do. However, if the wrong situation presents itself, your ideas and operating outside of protocol and regulation may be what saves others' lives!"

Sun then said, "If this is true, I will accompany you back to the Deep Space Station. If I like what I see, I will stay. However, if they tell me regulation is to be followed regardless of the circumstance then I will leave."

Owens laughing then replied, "You and me both Sun." The two then made their way to President Hays and the three departed for the Deep Space Station.

Once at the deep space station President Hays and Captain Owens took Sun Tu to his quarters. Now in front of his quarter's door Sun turned around and said, "I have many questions, and I would like to ask them now if you have the time." The two men a little fearful of what he may ask knew that they would have to withhold some information. They feared that if they told him everything he would simply turn around and go back to Japan. However, they would have to give him just enough information to spark his interest and make him want to stay and be part of the crew. To do this the two men told Sun that the mission was to go into the black hole and there were possibilities that the ship would not be able to return using the same route. If this were to happen, they would need Sun's expertise. As an extended mission would cause the ship to run out of fuel and alternate methods would need to be found to fuel the ship and there was also a possibility that an extended mission would end in the need for fabricated parts.

Upon hearing this Sun immediately told the two men that he would need to look at the engine the ship was to be fitted with and would need to know all of the engine specifics so that he could determine where and if changes could be made. He then continued on, in an almost psychotic rant, telling the two men that the parts used and capabilities already present would determine what could be accomplished in timed or emergency situation. The two men agreed that Sun's request was in the best interest of the mission.

Upon coming to this conclusion, they then told Sun that he would have immediate access to all mechanical systems the next day. As Sun was to be fitted for his uniform and have medical testing completed on him for the remainder of the day.

After hearing all of this Sun immediately asked when he would be introduced to the rest of the crew. President Hays at this point remained speechless. However, Captain

Owens did not. Captain Owens looked Sun Tu in the eyes and said, "You will be introduced to the rest of the crew when we pick them. The backbone of any ship is the captain. However, the beating heart of the ship lies in the hands of the chief mechanic. Which is exactly the reason you were the first individual picked to man Eclipse 8. Without a strong heartbeat there is no mission."

Chapter 5
The Botanist

After filling the chief engineer position, it was time to fill the botanist position. President Hays and Captain Owens knew that this role was just as important as the chief engineer role. As the head botanist would have to provide the crew with food after the initial supply of rations expired or was consumed. This individual would also need to ensure that plant life remained in good health, since there was a possibility that they may not be able to return to the Deep Space Station to get new seeds or replacement plants. If a plant ceased to exist there would be no possibility of bringing it back. A working knowledge of the systems within the atrium would be mandatory as well. Due to limited crew, there would not be enough mechanics among Eclipse 8 to move to the atrium to maintain its systems. Since the plants were also serving as a viable source of oxygen it made them even more important. If the plants within the atrium began to die, or an issue was experienced then it would directly affect the health of those on the ship, as their oxygen supply would be affected. In turn, the ships emergency systems would have to be used until new plants were grown or a new method was developed to restore the oxygen that was lost during the endeavor.

When the two men began their search for an individual to fill this role, they followed a different path than they did with Sun Tu. This time the two men began their search at the L.I.G.H.T. Academy. However, the two men could not pinpoint one individual person that possessed all the skills that would be necessary to benefit the crew. The first individual that the two men looked at was very good at starting plants and plant growth. However, the individual was not sufficient when it came to harvesting crops and using seeds from harvested crops to start new growth. In turn, this would end up leading to plants being removed from the ships inventory once all seeds had been planted.

The second individual that the men interviewed seemed to be a sure fit. However, when they tested the individual on a replica system, he proved to be inefficient with water conservation. Although he was adequate in terms of growing and harvesting crops, he kept depleting the water supply. The man would water the plants until the water supply was completely empty. At this point the plants would begin to die. Once the water was replenished then the plants would begin to grow again. However, the period that the plants had to go without water caused the harvest to be much smaller than it should have been and yielded less produce.

The third and final candidate they interviewed seemed to be the total package. He was very good when it came to maintenance of the crops. He even showed stellar potential when it came to harvesting crops and replanting. He knew everything that was necessary to keep the plant life in good health. However, when testing the individual, they decided to throw the candidate a curve ball. Captain Owens and President Hays caused a fault within the simulated atrium system. Instead of fixing the error though the candidate said the simulation was over. When the two asked him what he meant, he simply said that the system was broken and there was no one to work on it. Upon further questioning he then said he attended the academy to be a botanist not an engineer, and he would not work on the system.

After looking at candidates throughout the L.I.G.H.T. Academy the two men decided that they needed to take their endeavors elsewhere. That being said, the two men boarded a ship and headed to the United States. Once in the United States the two men searched every agricultural academy. However, everywhere the two men went they got the same answers. Most individuals told them that they had no interest in the mission, as they were looking for ways to solve the current issues, they were experiencing on earth. Other individuals told them they had never been off of the planet and would not know how to work the operating systems on the ship and did not have the time to learn how.

Now having little to no hope the two men began their journey back to the Deep Space Station. While aboard their return flight Captain Owens looked at President Hays and said, "Maybe we are looking at the wrong people. There are several people that we didn't interview or test. I feel that we have overlooked a perfect choice that was in plain sight."

President Hays then responded, "We have looked at all candidates within the L.I.G.H.T. Academy, and all of the agricultural academies throughout the United States. Where else can we look?" After sitting deep thought for several hours during their return flight though Captain Owens finally had an epiphany.

He immediately looked at President Hays and said, "We looked at the students within the L.I.G.H.T. Academy and the students within the academies in the United States. However, we didn't look at the professors."

President Hays then said, "You are one hundred percent right. When we get back to the Deep Space Station, we will shift our search to the professors that are already employed."

After arriving at the Deep Space Station, the two men immediately engaged in their search again. However, they did not immediately start interviewing the professors among the academy. Instead, the two men looked through the Academy archives for accomplishments and contributions that individuals had made to the academy. Upon reviewing everyone's records the two men found that one professor in particular had actually helped to invent and incorporate the system that was in place and to be used on Eclipse 8.

The individual professor that helped develop and emplace this system was Dr. John Red. Although this individual had never gone through the academy or been a L.I.G.H.T. employee, as a professor he had made a greater impact in his field than those that had attended over the years or currently worked on other ships. He also knew more than most men that were part of the agency or candidates when it came to botany and continued operations in austere environments. The problem that now remained though was, would Captain Owens and President Hays be able to convince the man to step down from his prestigious position as a professor and head of the botany division to take part in the mission.

Upon coming to the conclusion that this was the man that would best fit the position Captain Owens and President Hays went to talk to Mr. Red. However, when the two men greeted Mr. Red, he beat them to the punch. After introductions were complete Mr. Red immediately said, "I figure that the reason you are here is because you found no candidates that met your needs, and none that wanted to fill the position. I also imagine that after conducting research you found out I am the one that developed the system that is going to be used."

Captain Owens and President Hays in disbelief both smiled at this point. Then President Hays responded, "Sir, you would be correct in all accounts. We have interviewed individuals here at the Academy, but you already knew that. We also went to many of the agricultural colleges in the United States and found no one that was willing to learn about the system or even take the job for that matter. Most candidates said they only wanted to deal with the problems on earth. Even though I am pretty sure that is what we are doing as well. That being said, how would you feel about being the botanist to man Eclipse 8 on their upcoming mission?"

Mr. Red quickly responded, "Since I feel that you have actually worked to find a candidate, done your due diligence, and still ceased to find any qualified personnel, I will take the position. It is my responsibility as much as any other professor among this academy to present you with qualified personnel for all L.I.G.H.T. missions. Since I am unable to provide you with such a person, I will accept the responsibility. However, I will go as civilian personnel. I do not wish to become part of the Agency. I am also doing this because I feel an obligation to ensure that my system works correctly and all members of the crew are provided with food and adequate oxygen. If that requires me to be the one that looks after it, then that is what will happen." Captain Owens and President Hays looked to be speechless after the man's comments.

However, Captain Owens looked at the man and said, "We agree to your terms, sir, and we are honored to have you accompanying personnel on this mission. Just let us know how much time you need to prepare for the upcoming mission and how much time you will need to ready the atrium on the ship."

Mr. Red then responded, "I do not need training as I am the one that developed the system and I know all flaws, as well as, efficiency areas. That being said, I will continue to teach classes until the crew takes part in consolidated training. When that training starts, I will begin to ready the atrium and ensure that plants are providing fruit before the mission launches."

Chapter 6
The Chief Medical Officer

Although the men were far from having a full crew, they were beginning to feel a little relieved and accomplished. As they had been successful, or better yet, fortunate in their endeavors thus far. The two men initially believed that those they were attempting to recruit would not want to be part of the crew or the mission, because of the possibility of not being able to return. However, quite the opposite had been true. The individuals that the two men were attempting to recruit, which had evaded or declined being part of L.I.G.H.T. in the past, were now accepting offers, because of the uniqueness of the mission, and the possibility of not having to follow strict L.I.G.H.T. guidance and regulation.

Captain Owens and President Hays had now filled two of the most important positions. Positions that would have the greatest impact on the mission. If either of the two men they had already recruited were unable to do their job the crew would either starve, or the ship would cease to operate correctly. In either instance, life on Eclipse 8 would be greatly impacted and the mission would end up being a failure.

Now the task that the two were forged with was finding a chief medical officer. This individual much like the engineer and botanist though, would have to be able to operate in a manner that was not taught in the academy. They would have to be able to operate outside of protocol and regulation. They would have to be an individual that could think on their feet and react without having to refer to medical dictionaries or run scenarios through generators to determine possible outcomes. Because truth be told, if this individual was having to do their job something had already gone wrong.

This time though it didn't take long for an individual to come to mind. When the thought of a Chief Medical Officer was brought up Captain Owens immediately began to chuckle. He knew exactly what type of man they needed fill the position and right where to find him.

Seeing the look on Captain Owen's face and hearing his chuckle President Hays said, "By your chuckle I feel that you already have someone in mind."

Captain Owens then replied, "Yes, I do, and you know him, as well as, I do. However, you probably haven't seen him as much as I have."

President Hays now interested said, "Well who is it?"

Captain Owens said, "Wayne Green, the doctor that treats personnel injured at the Space Station Bar."

President Hays simply responded, "True, there is no better doctor for strange injuries not seen before. However, he hasn't manned a mission in about ten years. Do you think he will take the job?"

Captain Owens responded, "He will take the job if we present it to him the right way. The problem is going to be coming up with an elevator pitch that grabs his attention. One that pulls him into an unwinnable bet. Because in the end that is his type of game."

President Hays then asked, "Jake I think I am a little lost. What do you mean elevator pitch, grabbing his attention, and beating him at his own game?"

Captain Owens at this point, now with a semi-serious look on his face then responded, "He is an avid gambler in his down time. If we can come up with a good elevator pitch that gets him to bet on taking part in the mission and lose, he is ours. So, I hope you have a good poker face."

Now with a plan in mind the two men knew they would need to find the good doctor. Both knew that if he was not in the Deep Space Station Treatment Facility, he would be in the bar playing cards. Upon reaching the Treatment facility, the two found that it was Green's day off, so they then moved to the Space Station Bar. Upon entering the doors, the two immediately saw the man sitting at a table in the back corner of the bar with a few cadets and other members of the L.I.G.H.T. Agency. Seeing him, the two men made their way to his location. Once there, President Hays said, "Do you have room for one more."

However, Green immediately responded, "Too late to join the game boys but you are more than welcome to watch. We will be done here within the hour." Hearing this the two men moved away from the corner and started talking about another strategy that could be used. However, both men were drawing blanks.

President Hays then asked, "Do we really need to beat him at his own game, or do you think we can be the voice of reason and hope that it convinces him?"

41

Captain Owens then responded, "Sure we can try both ways. If for some reason he is deaf to the voice of reason, then we can always fall back on beating him in a good old-fashioned game of poker."

The two men having reached an agreement now waited on the man's game to come to a conclusion. It was almost exactly an hour later when Green stood up and shook his opponent's hand as he placed a large sum of cash in his pocket. As the doctor began to leave the bar President Hays summoned him to his location. Now standing next to the two men he responded, "To what do I owe the honor gentlemen?"

President Hays slightly hesitant then commented, "How would you feel about taking part in an upcoming mission?"

Wayne laughing at this then said, "I will have to pass. I have more than I can handle here every Thursday, Friday, and Saturday night. But I do thank you for the offer gentlemen."

Captain Owens now standing almost right beside the man responded, "What if one of us beat you at your own game."

Green quickly responded, "You now have my attention. What do you have in mind?"

Captain Owens smiling replied, "If one of us can beat you at a game of poker you man Eclipse 8."

Wayne then responded, "So what is in it for me if I win?" Captain Owens and President Hays now looking at each other knew they would have to think fast.

President Hays then replied, "If you win, then I will give you full retirement plus 50% on top of those wages."

Wayne without thinking said, "I will take those odds sir."

Immediately following the conversation, the three men sat back down at the table Wayne had just finished playing at. To make the odds even and to ensure that no one was cheating the men agreed to have an outsider deal the cards. Upon the start of the game Wayne was leading the charge, and from an outsider's view would quickly be winning what looked to be a one-sided game. As he had won 5 out of 7 hands played. However, Captain Owens was quite the card player himself and while watching the man had learned some of his tell signs. Tells that in the end would lead to him losing a large wager that was made. It was about three quarters of the way into the game when Captain Owens ended up with a high straight. Seeing his hand, and knowing that if he acted like he wasn't confident he could lead Wayne all in, he slowly did. In the end, leaving Wayne with only about five dollars in chips.

Wayne now having little to no money left at this point slightly chuckled and finished off the glass of jack and coke he had sitting in front of him. He knew that due to probability, the odds were finally stacked against him, he knew that he would have to go all in to even have a chance at a come back, and would still be relying on blind luck. Regardless he shrugged his shoulders and pushed what money he had left into the center of the table as the cards began to be dealt again. Afterwards he waited for Captain Owens to look at his hand. Once his opponent had looked at the cards, he was dealt he then slowly picked up his hand to reveal five low cards that were all off suit and knew that for once he had lost. Knowing this and to avoid embarrassment he then stood up, looked at the two men, and said, "I guess you have yourself a Chief Medical Officer. When does training start?"

Captain Owens looking at the man replied, "Training starts immediately; however, we do not have a full crew yet. So far, we have a botanist and a chief mechanic."

Hearing this Green then commented, "Who are the two filling those roles?"

President Hays responded, "Well the chief mechanic you wouldn't know, as he has never attended the academy, or been part of L.I.G.H.T. His name is Sun Tu. However, the botanist you do know, as he is a professor here at the L.I.G.H.T. academy."

Green then responded, "Which professor was crazy enough to leave his overcompensating pension here at the academy to go on a mission?"

President Hays then said, "Professor Red surprisingly, and thank god for that. We interviewed every candidate in the L.I.G.H.T. academy, the academies on earth, and even a number of professors here. He only volunteered for the mission because he knew we had run out of candidates and didn't want anyone messing up the system that he created."

Green at this point just nodded his head and then said, "Good man for the job. Has been overlooked quite a few times here at the academy. He will definitely get the job done. Only man I ever seen that cares more for plants than he does people. Definitely weird though. I saw him in the bar one day talking to a plant. I can't imagine it had much to say back to him, but hey to each their own. President Hays, Captain Owens, the honor of being a member of the crew is now mine, I guess. So, show me the way to where training will be held. However, I do have a couple of requests though."

Captain Owens hearing this then asked, "And what are those requests?"

Wayne responded, "I will be the one that decides how the medical bay is set up and the medical procedures that are to be followed in different situations." President Hays and Captain Owens had no problem with this request and both nodded and agreed with the man.

Upon which time Captain Owens looked at Wayne and said, "Well if you will follow us, we will introduce you to the other two members of the crew. After being introduced we will give you ample time to gather the things that you need or want to take with you before being confined to the training area."

Wayne then stated, "Oh, yeah! I almost forgot. If I go, my dog Storm goes with me. She is kind of my good luck charm."

President Hays to keep the man happy then said, "Wayne that will be fine. Any luck that can be added to the mission wouldn't hurt. I hope that everything goes off without a hitch, but at this point we are in uncharted waters."

With nothing more to say the men then left the bar and headed through the space station to meet the other members.

Chapter 7
The Weapon Specialist

A Mission that once seemed like it was going to be impossible to conduct due to the lack of crew members, and support was now beginning to look promising. Although, the crew was far from being filled and training had not yet begun. Captain Owens and President Hays were becoming more and more confident that they would be able to continue to fill crew member positions with the most capable individuals within their operating galaxy. The two men were beginning to feel that regardless of what happened after the initial launch the crew would be able to sustain life and continue on.

However, the two men now knew that it was time to stop focusing on what they had accomplished and focus on what they still needed to do, which was find a weapon specialist. This individual however, was more than just an individual that would ensure that all weapon systems were working. They would also be responsible for the ships shields and cloaking system, as all systems were closely related and would be operated out of the same central location within the ship. This in mind, President Hays and Captain Owens knew that they would have to take their search elsewhere as they did before. As the L.I.G.H.T. Academy did not employ weapons technicians or have classes for the field of weapon operations and technology. In the past, systems of this nature had never been needed for space exploration.

The first place that the two men went to look for individuals to fill this role was the military. However, sadly to their surprise all they could find were individuals that were specialized on specific types of weapon systems. They also found that in many cases the weapon systems that individuals were specialized on they were not actually able to work on. Upon finding this information out the two men came to the conclusion that they should look to the companies that the military purchased the weapons from. As individuals within these companies would know exactly how the weapon systems were constructed and how to keep them in operation.

The first company the two men looked to was Brass Incorporated. This business was one that had started out when conventional weapons were still in use. However, over the years the company had become one of the top manufacturers of laser weapon systems and specialized in laser operations and laser technology. The two men went through all of the company's departments and interviewed everyone that showed interest in their offer. However, they continued to come up short, as the only field that employees from Brass Incorporated could be of any assistance in was defensive laser systems. They had no operating knowledge when it came to the ships shields and cloaking device.

The next company that the two men went to in search of a worthy candidate was Apocalypse Industries. This company not only specialized in laser technology but was also on the rise for defensive shields. A technology that was growing among space stations. As this technology kept space stations safe when passing through asteroid belts. After interviewing several employees, the two men found a possible candidate. However, they felt that if they continued to search, they may find one individual that could tend to all of the systems in question. Instead of having to take on several individuals that only specialized in a couple of the systems.

The next company that President Hays and Captain Owens went to in search of a weapons specialist was Mechanical Engineering World Wide. This company not only specialized in laser technology but they also provided services in cloaking technology, and defensive shields. After interviewing several individuals, the two men came across an individual that claimed the best person to fill the position was actually his roommate in college. However, he said to interview this individual they would have to visit him in the Earth Federal Penitentiary. As that is where the individual had been located for the past five years. At the conclusion of the interview Captain Owens out of curiosity then asked, "So what exactly did he do to get placed in the Federal Penitentiary?"

The interviewee then laughed and said, "I will let you find that out on your own. However, his name is Gauge Latham."

After the interviewee left, President Hays looked at Captain Owens and said, "You are not seriously considering that we go to the Federal Penitentiary and interview this man are you."

Captain Owens then said, "We don't have to, I feel that his record will probably tell us everything that we need to know. If we look at his record and we are still curious then we can make it a point to go interview him."

President Hays laughing looked at Owens and then said, "Why not, I mean look at some of the people we already have going. They may not be the most socially accepted, but at least we know they will get the job done. The worst that can happen is we see that the individual is underqualified and have to continue looking."

The next day the two men went to Earth Law Enforcement Agency and asked to have the individuals record pulled so that they could review it. Upon asking the clerk for the record the clerk looked at them in a surprised manner and said, "Sure thing! Do you want only his adult record or would you like his juvenile record as well?"

The two men looked at each other in confusion at this point and then Captain Owens said, "Bring them both I am sure the files can't be that extensive."

The clerk then laughed and said, "Follow me gentlemen! It would probably be better to take you to his files other than bringing them to you." As the two men stepped into the file room the clerk pointed them to a shelf filled with boxes.

Captain Owens then said, "Which box is his file?"

The clerk again laughed and said, "The shelf is his file. It seems that he didn't reach his full potential until he was in college."

After looking at the shelf for several minutes in disbelief President Hays looked at Captain Owens and said, "Well I guess we better get to work reading. It looks like this is going to take a lot longer than we had expected." Both men then grabbed a box and started looking through the contents. Every once in a while, the two would look at each other and read a file off in disbelief. The first one that Captain Owens read aloud was a charge he was convicted of when he was five.

Captain Owens looked at President Hays and said, "When Gauge was five, he cloaked a washing machine that he had placed in the center of the road and let a car hit it."

Later President Hays said, "Well this was the last file and the reason that he ended up here."

Owens now curious then said, "Well read it out loud. After looking at some of these other files my curiosity is sparked."

President Hays cleared his throat and then began, "Mr. Latham's senior project landed him in here. Apparently, he was quiet the prankster. It seems that he stole a galactic police cruiser that he retro fitted with lasers and a cloaking device in his garage. When officers received word that he was the one that stole the vehicle they went to his home. The funny thing is, he is the one that tipped them off. Once they were at his residence, he shot a cruiser disabling it. He then played a game of cat and mouse. He would disable a cruiser at one location, cloak the vehicle and do the same at another location. It says here that he disabled and destroyed over half of the galactic fleet in a 16-hour period. They actually didn't catch him though, in the end he turned himself in."

Captain Owens then asked, "How is that a senior prank? Not much humor in all of that. Planks are supposed to be funny."

President Hays then said, "Well according to the court records he didn't fight any of the charges. He actually went into detail to explain how he obtained the car. The process he went through when retro fitting the vehicle. I mean he even explained the routes that he took when he was on his destruction escapade. Apparently, no one else was amused, but it said he was smiling and laughing throughout the whole trial. So either he has a very different sense of humor, or he is crazy. However, I don't think a crazy person puts that much thought into a crime that they are about to commit."

President Hays upon finishing the file then looked at Captain Owens and said, "I think you may have been right. I think that Gauge is the individual that we have been looking for. He may not be as funny as he thinks he is, but it seems like he is a genius in all the correct fields. Although the issue we will have now is getting him released into our custody."

Many weeks and several documents later President Hays and Captain Owens were able to convince the court and law systems to release Gauge into their custody. Upon meeting Gauge for the first time President Hays said, "Gauge, I am President Hays of the L.I.G.H.T. Agency."

Gauge immediately stopped him and said, "I know who you are and I know why you are here. You need me for your upcoming death mission. Which I will do as long as I get paid and it gets me out of here."

Captain Owens now confused looked at Gauge and said, "I am not sure how you know about the mission, especially being in this place. Or what you think you know about the mission, but I can promise you two things. The first thing is that you will get paid. The second, is that we will be getting you out of this place today. If you could follow us, we will get you to the Deep Space Station. Once we arrive, we can discuss mission specifics and job responsibilities after we introduce you to the rest of the crew." Following the two individuals' interaction, Captain Owens looked at President Hays and said, "I like this one. He reminds me of a young me. Full of piss and vinegar."

Chapter 8
The First Officer

All but two major roles had now been filled, and although each proved to be difficult and come with its own rigors the most arduous of the positions had yet to be filled. These two positions were the most important, not only in terms of mission accomplishment, but in terms of life expectancy for those aboard Eclipse 8. As these individuals' decisions would impact all those that served under them. The first of the two positions was that of the captain. This sole entity would need to be able to operate in all conditions without oversight or supervision. In many cases, he would need to be able to determine when doctrine and regulation would need to be followed and when it no longer pertained to the situations that they would be faced with. The second position, was that of the First Officer. Which would need to be the voice of reason. This individual would need to be able to question certain decisions made by the captain. He would need to be able to accomplish this in a tactful manner that would not cause those assigned under them to question the captains ability to lead though.

President Hays and Captain Owens believed that the individual that they chose to fill the First Officer position should already have time as a Captain or First Officer on another ship. The two men felt this way because in many cases it was easier to accept advice from someone that had been faced with similar circumstances or that had been forced to make difficult decisions in the past under pressure or when experiencing duress. They also believed this because if the worst were to happen and the acting commander was killed, it would be an easy transition for them to take over and continue operations.

President Hays and Captain Owens did not begin interviewing individuals immediately for the position though. Instead, as they had done many times in the past, they began reviewing records of those employed by the L.I.G.H.T Academy and those that had performed operations for the agency. The two men meticulously went through flight logs and overall records. While doing this, they also reviewed files and attachments within the records to see what individual responses were when multiple candidates had been faced with the same or similar situations. As past experiences, could help if the individuals were faced with similar issues. Especially if only one of the many candidates were able to think outside the box and still get the same results.

After countless hours and several days, the two men had narrowed their search down to six individuals. All individuals had been very close in terms of overall performance, and had all encountered situations that had it not been for their quick decision-making skills would have lost not only a ship but their crew as well. The six men that they chose as candidates were two first officers and four captains. However, two of the selected candidates were retired.

Knowing that two of the men selected were retired, President Hays and Captain Owens planned on starting their interviews with these men. As the two knew that they would either receive interest immediately or be turned away without hesitation. The first to be interviewed was Captain Riley. Upon arrival at Captain Riley's house, President Hays and Captain Owens were greeted with kindness. The two men sat down with the retired Captain and stated their purpose for being there. They figured that the best method in this case was to be very decisive and avoid misleading anyone. After stating the situation Captain Riley smiled and said, "Although I would love to be the First Officer for this mission my time with L.I.G.H.T. is over. I flew for L.I.G.H.T. for 27 years with distinction. Every mission not knowing if I would return to my family. I missed birthdays, anniversaries, and even my children's weddings. That being said, I will have to pass on this opportunity. It is time that I give back to my family as they have sacrificed for me for several years."

After hearing Captain Riley's response President Hays and Captain Owens simply looked at the retired Captain smiling and Captain Owens said, "I thank you for your time, sir, and I also thank you for your distinguished service. It is because of men like you we have been able to succeed where others have failed." Afterwards President Hays and Captain Owens shook the man's hand and once again embarked on their search.

The next individual on the list was retired Captain Buckley. However, upon arrival to Captain Buckley's home the two men were not greeted with the same hospitality. Instead, as soon as the men knocked on the door Captain Buckley's wife answered and stated, "If this has anything to do with the L.I.G.H.T. Agency and my husband he is retired. He already gave you half of our marriage and slept with two of your lady officers."

At this point President Hays tried to calm the woman and said, "Ma'am—" However, he was cut off by the loading of an old Mossberg shotgun before he could finish.

Mrs. Buckley looked at President Hays after loading the weapon and said, "You have until I get to the count of ten and then I start firing. Maybe I hit you and maybe I don't. The question is, is that a risk you are willing to take."

Captain Owens at this point looked at the woman and said, "Ma'am, there is no need for violence, a simple no would have sufficed. We will be on our way and give your husband our regards."

The search was now narrowed to two individuals currently serving as first officers and two individuals serving as captains. President Hays now looking at Captain Owens said, "How about we try the first officers this time? It might lessen the chance of a weapon being pulled on us. Or, it could increase it. We all know how new first officers are." Captain Owens at this point simply laughed, smiled ear to ear, and then shook his head yes. With that, the next individual on the list was First Officer Loui of the Galactic L.I.G.H.T. operations post.

For this interview the two men would have to travel to the Galactic L.I.G.H.T. operations post as members of the outpost were not allowed to leave. However, they conducted the interview in an unconventional manner. This time the two men had the first officers captain in the interview room with them. Captain Owens began the conversation this time by saying, "Loui do you know why we are here?"

Loui immediately responded, "I have a feeling it has to do with the upcoming mission but I don't know anything other than that really."

Captain Owens looked at the man and said, "We are looking for a First Officer for Eclipse 8 that is competent and has the ability to lead if put in a situation where it is required."

Loui looked at Captain Owens and said, "I am already a First Officer on a distinguished ship. Why would I leave one crew for another?"

Captain Owens then said, "I understand what you are saying. However, operating in a mission such as this one would open doors for you and give you a leg up on others filling the same role. It would most certainly ensure that you gain command of your own ship."

Loui paused for a moment and then looked at his current Captain and said, "Sir what are your thoughts on this matter?"

His captain looked at him and said, "Well I feel that you are perfectly capable and possess the skills necessary to command your own ship. However, I am sure President Hays and Captain Owens are the subject matter experts in this field. The decision overall is in your hands, but I will support you regardless of what decision you make."

First Officer Loui then looked at President Hays and Captain Owens and said, "I thank you for the opportunity that you are giving me, however, I would like to stay with my current command. As I am not willing to trade off one crew for another. Their life is in my hands and that is where it will remain." Both men just nodded graciously and exited the operations bridge and made their way back to President Hays quarters.

As soon as the two men arrived at President Hays quarters, President Hays reached into his liquor cabinet and pulled out a bottle of whiskey and poured two shots. Immediately handing one of them to Captain Owens. He then looked at Captain Owens and said, "Though our journey is a hard one, it is worth it in the end. It is us that must succeed in not only finding individuals to fill positions for this mission, but ensure that they are fully qualified. Mankind is counting on us!"

Captain Owens finishing off his whiskey then replied, "Well that being said, after this we better get to it. We still have a First Officer and a Captain to find." Afterwards the two men began their search once more.

The next individual that the two men would interview would be First Officer Lead of the 5th Apache Galactic Cruiser. As they did with First Officer Loui the two men pulled the captain and First Officer into the ships bridge. Once there, President Hays started by saying, "I will get straight to the point as we are all very busy men. I am here to recruit First Officer Lead for our upcoming Eclipse 8 Mission. It is his decision on whether he accepts the offer or denies it. However, as a former Captain, I expect you to support his decision as I would if I were in your shoes."

At this point President Hays and Captain Owens got a response they were not expecting. First Officer Lead at this point looked at the two men and said, "The captain and I have already discussed the mission at hand. I told the captain that I was interested in taking part in the mission even if it was only as a bridge hand. I feel that space exploration is getting ready to take a new turn and I would like to be there when it happens. That being said, I will accept your offer."

Captain Owens at this point responded, "I honor your forwardness and your willingness to take part in the unknown."

President Hays then stated, "Captain is there anything that we can do for you to help with the loss of your First Officer?"

The captain looked at him and said, "As far as manning I will be okay. I have another individual that is ready to step up and fill a more demanding role. However, I do ask that you place someone in charge of him that respects him as much as I do, not only as a First Officer but as a man."

President Hays looked at the captain and said, "Trust me I will ensure that is exactly what happens. On a further note, if you would like to accompany us, I will take you back to where the rest of the crew is being held so introductions can be made."

Chapter 9
The Captain

There was now only one position left to fill. The most important position among the ship, the "captain". Before engaging in a search this time President Hays looked at Captain Owens and said, "I have four individuals in mind for this position."

Captain Owens looked back at him and said, "You have not led us astray yet. I trust your judgement and will do my best to assist you in any manner that I can."

It was at this moment that President Hays looked at Captain Owens and said, "The four candidates are Captain Moon of the Integra, Captain Alley of the Alyssa, Captain Foray of the Apollo 91, and Captain Serine of the War Machine."

Captain Owens looked at President Hays and said, "Those are all excellent choices. I would have picked the same individuals, as all have served with honor and distinguished themselves among their peers."

The first candidate was Captain Moon. Upon arriving at the Integra, President Hays asked all crew members to exit the bridge. Captain Owens took lead this time by saying, "Obviously it is no mystery why we are here. We have a very important upcoming mission and we are looking for the best of the best to Captain the ship. However, if you say yes know at this point the crew has already been chosen based on talent and expertise. So, you would not be picking your own crew."

Captain Moon at this point looked at the two men and said, "I appreciate your straight forwardness. However, I will have to pass on this opportunity. I believe that to abandon my crew would not only be wrong of me but would be irresponsible as a Captain. Had I not been in charge of a ship at this moment I would have taken the offer with honor. I am sorry if I have offended you, but this is where I stand on the offer."

Captain Owens then responded, "You do realize that this is a once in a lifetime opportunity that could revolutionize space exploration, right?"

Captain Moon then said, "I understand and this decision was not one that was made lightly. I spent countless hours debating on if I should take the offer if it was presented to me. However, leaving my current ship and my crew would leave me with a heavy heart."

President Hays then said, "Well sir I thank you for your time and still expect great things from you in the future. If you need anything from me or the L.I.G.H.T. Agency do not hesitate to let me know and I will ensure that every effort is made to ensure that it happens."

After meeting with Captain Moon, the two men made their way to the Alyssa where they were to meet with Captain Alley. Upon arriving at the Alyssa, the two men found that the ship was currently docked at the Deep Space

Station. The crew had just returned from a six-month tour, where they were taking part in resource resupply missions.

Leading the interview, President Hays said, "First off, I thank you for the efforts that you made on your last expedition. I wish that results would have been better, however, I know that we cannot change fate. Now for the reason that I am here. Captain Alley I am here to recruit you to be the captain of Eclipse 8."

At this point Captain Alley looked at the two men and said, "From what I understand you have already chosen a crew."

President Hays responded with, "Yes, Captain, a crew has been chosen based off of capabilities and expertise in selected fields."

Captain Alley then looked at President Hays and said, "Why did L.I.G.H.T. pick the crew? Should it not have been the captains decision who filled the roles on his ship? Does L.I.G.H.T. Command not trust the captains that were appointed by them?"

Captain Owens now disgruntled and angered by the man's attitude spoke above the two men and said, "Well in past occurrences, captains would pick their crew based on how good of friends they were. A system that has become known as the good old boys' system. Leaving less than qualified personnel in positions and hoping for the best. We came here because we felt that your past accomplishments and track record made you a good fit. The crew of Eclipse 8 was picked with the same merit. That being the case, it is a very straight forward question. Captain Alley, do you accept the offer that is being presented to you now? Are you willing to accept the role of captain of Eclipse 8? Or should we move on? Because with the attitude you currently have, you shouldn't even be in charge of this ship."

Captain Alley now staring at Owens intensely with an angered look on his face replied, "I don't even know why you are here. You were pulled from your position because you failed to obey the orders of those placed over you. You shouldn't even be here."

President Hays then said, "Well Captain I have made my decision. I feel that you are not the right person for the position. If it wasn't for your previous outstanding service, I would say that you are not worthy or fit to be in command of any vessel. However, everyone is entitled to their opinion. I would have thought sitting in that chair though, you would have learned some sort of tact. If you have, you have failed to exercise it. This time I will overlook your rudeness. However, next time you speak to me or anyone else accompanying me in the manner you have today, I will ensure that you are never placed in command of anything again and relieved if you are in command." Following his comment President Hays and Captain Owens said nothing, they simply stood up and exited the ship's bridge.

After exiting, President Hays looked at Captain Owens and said, "I want to thank you for assisting me, as I know it has not been an easy thing for you to do. However, he was wrong in the comments that he made and had no right to speak the way he did. For that I do apologize. He is speaking out of ignorance and arrogance."

Captain Owens then said, "We all make decisions in life. The decisions that I made, I can live with. I feel that I did the right thing. Comments are made to me on a continuous basis, and over the years I have learned to take those comments with a grain of salt. However, we still have more people to interview and not a lot of time to do so."

The next Captain to be interviewed was Captain Foray of Apollo 91. Upon arrival to Apollo 91 however the men were not greeted by Captain Foray instead they were greeted by his Chief Medical Officer. Upon being greeted by the chief medical officer Captain Owens asked, "Where is Captain Foray? He was made aware of our meeting with him, correct?"

The chief medical officer then said, "He was made aware and he wants to meet with you. However, I have confined him to quarters as on our last expedition he contracted Space Infused Body Toxic Shock."

President Hays then asked, "How did this happen and what do you expect the recovery time to be?"

The chief medical officer then replied, "When he went to the surface of Nebula 27 on a landing party his space suit was torn on a surface rock. However, the self-sealant system did not react the way that it was designed to. In turn, he breathed in toxic gases from the planet's surface. As far as recovery time it can be anywhere from four weeks to seven months."

President Hays in disbelief looked at the chief medical officer and said, "Well maybe we can talk another time. However, in the meantime ensure that Captain Foray makes a speedy recovery. L.I.G.H.T. and myself are counting on you."

After leaving Captain Owens said, "Well it is on to our last hope now. However, I have full confidence that Captain Serine will accept the offer."

President Hays responded with, "Even if he doesn't accept the offer, I am sure that there are other options at our disposal." Upon arrival to the War Machine the two men were greeted immediately by Captain Serine. Captain Serine after greeting the men took them to his quarters.

Upon entering the room, he looked at the two men and said, "This must be an important matter or you would not be here. And as far as you Captain Owens I have not had the opportunity to meet you but it is a pleasure."

Upon finishing his statement President Hays looked at him and said, "Captain Serine I am here to ask you how you would feel about taking command of Eclipse 8 for the upcoming space exploration mission."

Captain Serine at this point smiling said, "If L.I.G.H.T. and yourself feel that I am ready for command of such a mission I will accept gladly." It was several minutes before anything else was said.

Then President Hays looked at Captain Serine and said, "If you were faced with the decision of disobeying an order to save a human life or obeying the order and in turn sentencing a man to death that you could have saved what would you do."

Captain Serine puzzled said, "Well, Sir, it is my duty to follow the orders of those appointed over me. So even though I wouldn't agree with the decision I would do what I was commanded to do. In the absence of that guidance, I would follow L.I.G.H.T. protocol and regulation."

President Hays with a sigh then responded, "Sir I thank you for your time and I will be in touch with you."

Upon leaving Captain Owens and President Hays remained silent. The silence was not broken until President

Hays looked at Captain Owens and said, "Upon arriving at the Deep Space Station, I would like it if you accompanied me to my quarters. Where we can further our search for a qualified individual to take command of Eclipse 8."

Captain Owens nodded and then said, "Yes, Sir." Upon arriving at President Hays quarters, President Hays once again went to his bar and opened the doors. However, this time he reached as far back in the cabinet as he could and pulled a wooden box from the back. Afterwards he placed it on the counter and opened it up. Captain Owens curious then asked, "What's in the box?"

President Hays looked at him and smiled and then said, "Something that has been passed down through ten generations of my family. It is only brought out for very special occasions."

Captain Owens then said, "Well what is the special occasion? We are still short a Captain right now." President Hays hearing Captain Owens did not acknowledge, instead placed two ice cubes in each glass and then filled them to the halfway point. After pouring the drinks he walked over to where Captain Owens was and handed him a glass and sat in the chair adjacent to him.

Again, Captain Owens at this point asked, "So you still haven't said what the special occasion is."

President Hays then said, "The whole time I had you looking for a crew and a captain I was trying to see if you were the same man that saved my life so many years ago."

Captain Owens then said, "You can change habits, but not the person that you are. But why were you trying to find out if I had changed?"

President Hays then responded, "I was never really looking for a Captain. I already had one in mind. The person that I have wanted to Captain Eclipse 8 has been you since we picked the first crew member. You are passionate about not only your ship but those that serve under you. It is a feature that very few Captains possess. It is because of that I am asking you Captain Owens, will you Captain Eclipse 8 despite your thoughts in the beginning?" Captain Owens sat in disbelief for a long time before responding.

He then said, "I will sir, however, know if the worst should happen on this mission, I will put human life before the ship."

President Hays then said, "Well then it is done! Captain Owens you are now in command of Eclipse 8 feel free to train the men as you feel necessary and make changes you feel necessary. I feel that you are the most capable and the best fit for the job." After saying this both men raised their glasses touched them together and began to slowly sip the aged whiskey that President Hays had poured.

Chapter 10
Training and
Mission Preparation

All of the major positions of the ship had now been filled. The remainder of the lower-level positions would be filled by those that were top of their class throughout the academy and volunteered, and few others from various outside agencies and colleges that met mandatory requirements identified by L.I.G.H.T. All individuals were to immediately be moved to Deep Lunar Space Station Bravo where they would begin their rigorous testing and tireless training. Once there all personnel would be broken down into their specific areas of operation for the initial or first weeks of training and would only conduct operations with individuals in their sectors. In the weeks to follow however training would progress and other sectors of the ship would conduct operations with each other. This would continue until the entire ship as a whole was conducting operations. Once the entire ship was conducting operations as a whole then they would be given different simulations which they would have to overcome or adapt too.

At the start of training, as with any new operation, times were tough and obstacles were overcome through hard lessons learned. In some situations, operations barely moved along at all and almost came to a complete stop. It was during this time that individuals commonly spoke out or had arguments with one another. In some cases, these verbal altercations ended in physical conflict. However, over time individuals learned to work with one another. Each day finding out or learning what areas they excelled in and what areas they struggled in. In the end, resulting in each area of the ship working like a finely tuned machine.

After each area of the ship was able to work within itself other sectors of the ship were integrated into each other's training and operations. Much like the beginning phases, being rough at first, until individuals learned to work with one another and in some cases rely on each other. Learning how each sector could prove beneficial to the other, the ship grew as a whole, until all sectors were working together. However, no member of the crew had actually worked or been aboard Eclipse 8 yet.

In the weeks to follow, Eclipse 8 was finally finished. However, the transition from a training environment to the actual work environment was not an easy one. When the crew finally manned Eclipse 8 and began to conduct training operations on the ship to ensure that all systems were operational, many flaws were found. It was through immense teamwork that the obstacles were able to be overcome. In some cases, entire operating systems actually had to be replaced. However, working all of the system errors out and ensuring that systems were operational now would help lessen the chance of problems occurring on the actual mission.

After 18 weeks of rigorous training and ensuring that systems were operational it was finally time to conduct mock or test missions. During these test missions the crew would be given situations that they may encounter. In some cases, the tasks were accomplished with absolutely no problems and in other instances it took many attempts to overcome the problem sets that they were faced with. Captain Owens however would not let the crew rest until they were able to accomplish all tasks. Whether it took the crew of Eclipse 8 hours or days failure was not an option.

After all training regimes had been completed and Captain Owens, as well as, L.I.G.H.T. Command felt that the crew of Eclipse 8 was fully capable and mission ready it was time to reattach Deep Space Station Bravo to the Deep Space Station and begin final preparations for the mission. After the ship was reattached Captain Owens spoke with President Hays and asked him if he could give his crew a five-day pass before they did final system checks before embarking on their mission. President Hays granted the pass gladly as he knew that the crew may have an uncertain future. Both men felt that the five-day pass was the least that could be done for the bravery the men and women had shown volunteering for the mission.

While all crew members were on pass one man remained with Eclipse 8. Captain Owens stayed at Eclipse 8 to ensure that everything was in order, and that things would go smoothly upon the crews return. While everyone was gone the ship was filled with food and supplies to last at least one year. In some areas more than a year's worth of supplies was able to be stored. Captain Owens was also conducting planning with military forces during this time period. Ensuring that all Military members were aware that he was the final deciding authority in all situations and that only if the ship and crew were in a state of survival or eminent danger would the military forces aboard be able to take charge of the ship. He also briefed these individuals on what was expected of them while they were aboard the ship, as well as, accompanying landing parties.

On the fifth day crew members starting arriving back to the ship in the late evening. One by one Captain Owens ensured that he greeted each one as they returned and ensured that they gave a proper goodbye to their families. Turning several individuals around until he was sure that they did so. After all crew members were aboard the ship, he instructed them to get as much sleep as they could for the final systems checks the following day.

The next morning operations started early. Every system had to be tested before the ship would be allowed to initiate departure from the Space Station. Every member of the crew also had to be tested to ensure that they were in good health before departing. As if one person was sick it could in turn cause an epidemic among the ship.

After several hours of testing the operations systems and electrical systems Eclipse 8 was blessed off on to depart the space station the following morning. Also, only four individuals had to be removed from the ship due to medical reasons. However, none of the individuals were pertinent to operations and were easily replaced. The next morning would be the day all members of the crew had been preparing for and fearing since the day they volunteered to take part in the mission.

After all testing was done President Hays boarded Eclipse 8 and went to Captain Owens quarters where he waited on him until he was done with commanding operations preparation on the bridge of the ship. When Captain Owens entered his quarters, he was surprised to see him there. After noticing President Hays, Captain Owens asked, "To what do I owe the honor Sir."

President Hays responded, "I know that the mission you are about to embark on has never been attempted before and that no ship has ever entered a black hole. However, I came to wish you luck and to ask a favor of you."

Captain Owens replied, "Sure President Hays, what favor?"

President Hays then said, "If science fails us and you are not able to come back the way you embark on your mission. Do not stop looking for a way back. Continue to look after the well-being of your crew and continue to look for a way to get them back to their family. Also, if conflict is encountered be the man that I know you are and try to resolve it without the use of violence."

Captain Owens then responded, "Sir, the crew is and always will be my first priority and no matter what we will return back to the Deep Space Station one way or another. As far as conflict, if a conflict is encountered, I will do what I can to ensure that it is eliminated in the most civil manner available." In closing the two men shook hands and President Hays hugged Captain Owens before exiting his quarters at which time he looked at the man and said, "Godspeed."

Chapter 11
3,2,1...Disengage

As morning came anticipation grew. Many crew members became nervous as their future was uncertain. Although all had faith in L.I.G.H.T. Command, L.I.G.H.T. command itself was unsure of how the mission would go. As 0900 hours approached all personnel manned their positions for their 1000 pre-check before departing the space station. If there were flaws within any operating system, the mission would be delayed until the issue could be resolved. However, if all checks went flawlessly Eclipse 8 would begin the countdown for detachment from the Deep Space Station and their journey into the black hole would begin.

The time was now 1000 hours and L.I.G.H.T. Command began their checks with Eclipse 8. The first area to be checked was the engine deck.

President Hays knowing the importance of the mission oversaw all checks with Chief Mechanic Sun Tu. One by one President Hays asked Sun Tu to start up all operating systems, and Sun Tu complied until all systems were running. After all systems were up President Hays had Sun Tu then conduct a digital check of the systems to ensure that they were operating flawlessly. As the engine was the heart of the ship and without it the ship would fall lifelessly through space.

After all systems were checked on the engine deck L.I.G.H.T. Command then began to have the ships bridge check all electrical systems. One by one, operators complied. Slowly they turned off each system and yelled, "System has been powered down and is offline at this time." Then when given the command they would begin the same sequence in reverse order and yelling, "System power has been engaged. Operating system is up and 100% functional."

The next area to be checked was the ships weapon systems. Although the ship would not be able to physically check the laser systems as they were docked. The first system to be checked was the ships cloaking capabilities. That being said, President Hays gave Weapons Specialist Gauge Latham the command to initiate cloaking. Gauge did so immediately, leaving the ship completely invisible as it remained docked to the Deep Space Station. Next President Hays told Gauge to initiate the ships defensive shield. As Gauge did so, you could not only not see the ship, but it now had a protective field around it that was able to absorb or disintegrate charges or munitions fired at the ship.

Now that all major systems had been checked President Hays came over the ships intercom system and said, "Captain Owens all major systems are a go at this time. Now we request that you conduct checks on a level-by-level basis. Upon completion and your command, we will initiate countdown for departure of the Deep Space Station."

Captain Owens then replied, "President Hays I acknowledge all, and we will begin checks immediately."

Captain Owens then looked at First Officer Lead and said, "First Officer Lead begin level checks. Once all level checks are complete inform me so that I can have Deep Space Command begin countdown and disengagement procedures."

One by one, First Officer Lead checked all levels. After all levels acknowledged their readiness, First Officer Lead looked at Captain Owens and said, "Sir all levels are a go and we are prepared to begin disengagement procedures." Upon hearing this Captain Owens called Deep Space Station Command and informed President Hays.

President Hays then came over the ships intercom system one last time saying, "Ladies and Gentlemen of Eclipse 8, today you begin your voyage into the unknown. Although we may not be with you physically, we will always be with you at heart. That being said, I hope that this one-year voyage leads to not only great success for the crew, but mankind as well. However, if the worst happens and you are unable to return or contact L.I.G.H.T. Command or the Deep Space Station, I expect all members of the crew to support one another and assist Captain Owens and First Officer Lead. If contact is made with other life, I expect all members of Eclipse 8 to facilitate peaceful communication and create working partnerships. In hopes of bettering the current situation that we face. In closing, I wish all of you the best of luck and a safe return, Godspeed!"

Seconds after the President Hays's transmission L.I.G.H.T. Command and the Deep Space Station once again came over the intercom and said, "Disengagement will begin in 3, 2, 1."

When L.I.G.H.T. Command and the Deep Space Station hit 1, Captain Owens looked at First Officer Lead and said, "Disengage the space docking arm and set our course for the Nexus 12 point of entry." First Officer Lead immediately complied disengaging the space docking arm from the Deep Space Station.

As the course was entered into the ships navigation system, the ship slowly turned, eventually to reveal the black hole Eclipse 8 was to enter. Leaving all crew members speechless. Although this is the point all crew members had been training for it was a moment that none were prepared for. Many thoughts of an uncertain future passed through everyone's head. Some crew members sat thinking that the mission would go flawlessly and they would return in exactly one year with a new found hope for mankind. While others sat wondering if the ship would be ripped apart as they passed through the black hole.

As the ship neared the black hole Captain Owens told First Officer Lead to stop the ship while he made a transmission to all crew members. After coming to a stop Captain Owens came over the intercom system and said, "All members of the crew prepare for the unknown, we are now about to become travelers to a new destination. As we enter the black hole ensure that you are continuously monitoring your assigned systems. If any problems are encountered report them to the bridge immediately. We will begin entrance in T minus five minutes." As the transmission ended all crew members immediately began conducting last minute checks before engaging in an activity that had never been attempted by a human being. At the end of the five minutes Captain Owens looked at First

Officer Lead and said, "Officer Lead at this time engage the ships engines and begin entrance of the black hole."

The ship at this point began to slowly creep forward. Once near the black hole there was no stopping though. The black hole immediately began to pull the ship forward. At which point the ship was lost to the strength of the black hole's magnetic pull. Captain Owens at this point looked at First Officer Lead and said, "May God be with us as we enter the Unknown." Seconds later to everyone's surprise the ship was safely on the other side of their entrance point.

Once on the other side of the black hole Captain Owens came back over the intercom and informed all crew members that they had safely passed through to their destination and that they were once again to conduct system checks and report to the bridge. After all checks were complete Captain Owens began his first transmission to L.I.G.H.T. Command and the Deep Space Station. Captain Owens now on the ships command interface began his transmission, "President Hays and fellow L.I.G.H.T. Command personnel, we have successfully entered the black hole and have sustained no casualties or damage to the ship. We are now awaiting your command to begin our mission."

Several minutes later President Hays returned contact by saying, "I am glad that there were no complications and Captain Owens you are now in full control of the ship the crew is now at your disposal."

Captain Owens now in full control looked at First Officer Lead and said, "Officer Lead begin charting the solar system to determine our destination. Destination will be based off of which planets prove to have the most essential resources. Also begin a scan to ensure that there are no hostile threats in the immediate area. Lastly, ensure that our cloaking device is activated and the ships defensive shield is up until we determine that there are no threats and we have completed the navigational chart. From now until ordered otherwise we are to remain at a sense of readiness. As we do not know what we may encounter at this point."

First Officer Lead immediately complied with the captain's orders calling to Weapons Specialist Latham and saying, "Engage the ships cloaking and defensive systems. Once systems are operational inform the bridge so that navigational charting can begin." Seconds later Weapons Specialist Latham called back informing that all systems were up and working flawlessly. First Officer Lead then gave the order on the bridge for personnel to begin navigational charting.

Chapter 12
The First Exploration

Because the current solar system had never been explored all planets would have to be named. That being said, experts among the ship began labeling each planet with a corresponding letter and number. Labeling the planets in sequential order of importance. Beginning with A1 and continuing from that point. The first planet to be explored "A1" was of importance because there were signs of vegetation and water on the planet's surface. However, this would not be able to be verified until a landing party arrived on the planet's surface. As all information provided was from external scans that were conducted.

Travel to planet A1 would not be a speedy trip however. As the planet was about a one-month journey from the ship's current location. This time period would prove beneficial though as it would allow the crew to continue to label planets, as well as, allow systems flaws that were encountered to be corrected and members of the ship time to settle for the long journey ahead. This time also allowed initial decisions to be made before the crew actually stepped foot on the planet's surface.

The first thing that needed to be accomplished was a landing party needed to be established. The landing party however could not just consist of anyone. The individuals on the landing party would need to be able to take samples and test all substances gathered on the planet's surface. Individuals within this party would also need to be able to make decisions on if the planet would in fact be able to be inhabited or if it could prove useful to L.I.G.H.T. Command. Lastly, as always it would need to be determined that no danger was present. As the main priority of the Captain was ensuring that members of Eclipse 8 stay safe from harm and fit for duty.

Captain Owens while traveling to A1 began identifying personnel that the landing party would consist of. The first personnel that Captain Owens identified were scientists among the ship that specialized in minerals and raw materials. These individuals would be responsible for collecting core and resource samples from the planet's surface and determining their use. They would also have to identify if any of the resources could prove to be harmful to human life. While identifying personnel that would accompany the landing party in this field Captain Owens determined that key personnel should not accompany the party. As if anything happened to key personnel it could prove to be detrimental to the mission.

Next Captain Owens needed to identify medical personnel that would accompany the landing party. Medical personnel identified would be responsible for a number of different things. Obviously the first thing that medical personnel would be responsible for is monitoring landing party's vital signs to ensure that no member of the landing party had adverse reactions to the conditions they found themselves in. The next area that these personnel would prove useful in was the study of lifeforms found on the planet. If any were present. Medical personnel would take any living organism they found (if it was not intelligent life), study the life form, and then dissect it to find out the layout of the lifeform's anatomy.

The next personnel to be identified would be military personnel that would accompany the landing party. Although no threat was detected at this point, the landing party needed to be ready for any situation. These personnel would be responsible for providing security and safety for those that set foot on the planet's surface. In the case of a life threating situation military personnel would take control of the landing party and return to the ship for further action to be determined and a situational debrief.

The last individual to be chosen for the landing party was the officer that would be appointed over surface operations. Captain Owens felt it was best if he did not accompany the party however. If something were to happen while he was with the landing party on the planet's surface and the party was unable to return to the ship, decisive actions may be delayed. Instead, Captain Owens felt it best to send his First Officer. As First Officer Lead was more than capable of handling any situation that presented itself in a reasonable manner, while at the same time not affecting overall operations.

As the ship neared planet A1 the landing party prepared itself and boarded the Eclipse Voyager. Which was a small ship that was able to land on any surface. The Eclipse Voyager was also fitted with holding tanks for lifeforms, resources, and raw materials that were gathered. Once on the surface the landing party would have twelve hours to collect whatever they could. At the conclusion of the twelve hours the landing party would return to Eclipse 8 with their findings so that further research could be conducted. However, the landing party would not be allowed to join the general population of the ship until they spent another twelve-hour time period in a medical holding area to ensure that they did not suffer from any unseen side-affects that may have been caused from being on the unknown planet's surface.

Eclipse 8 now outside of A1's atmosphere instructed the Eclipse Voyager personnel to conduct landing party operations. Complying, Eclipse Voyager exited the Eclipse 8 landing bay and made their slow decent to the planet's surface. Once on A1 the landing party did not immediately exit the craft though. Instead, the landing party began analyzing the planets atmospheric composure and running scans of the immediate area to ensure that when they exited the craft they were not faced with a life and death situation, as well as, conducting scans to see if any lifeforms could be detected.

After about an hour the atmospheric scan was complete. To everyone's surprise the planet's atmosphere was primarily made of oxygen. However, there were traces of lithium and sulfur. Scientists among the landing party given these facts, and the small traces of secondary elements present, determined that it would be safe to remove their suit headgear upon exiting the craft. First Officer Lead however disagreed and stated that everyone would remain in full suit until they boarded the Eclipse Voyager for their return to Eclipse 8. Minutes later the environmental scan came back and showed that there were no detectable lifeforms within the area.

After all scans were complete, First Officer Lead gave the command to open the crafts doors so that further research could be conducted. As soon as he gave this command one of the four military personnel accompanying the party dropped the crafts rear door. Allowing all four military personnel to exit the craft and begin clearing the immediate area. After clearing the area, the military personnel signaled the rest of the crew to exit the craft. To everyone's surprise the surface of the planet was beautiful and untouched by man. There were forms of vegetation as far as the eye could see. Although they could not see any signs of water on the planet's surface.

Now that all personnel had excited the craft, it was time to get to work. Scientists and personnel immediately began to walk around and collect samples and fulfill the duties which they were sent to the planet's surface to conduct. About seven hours into operations one of the scientists looked at First Officer Lead and said, "Sir we have been on the planet's surface for seven hours and encountered no threats. We have also collected multiple samples of resources and minerals. Although there are many more samples that need to be taken. Sir, with your permission, I would like to remove my headgear and test the planets breathable oxygen supply."

First Officer Lead very hesitant then replied, "I will give one and only one of you permission to remove your headgear. If that individual doesn't experience any adverse results from removing their headgear, I will allow everyone else to do the same."

After two more hours had passed it was discovered that the scientist was in fact correct, and the planet's breathable oxygen could be circulated through the human system without causing any problems. First Officer Lead seeing this then gave the rest of the landing party permission to take off their suits' headgear.

The landing party continued to conduct operations for one more hour, until the unexpected happened. About an hour after all personnel had removed their headgear one of the military personnel on the landing party slapped his neck and said, "Wow, something just bit me." Upon hearing this one of the medical personnel ran over to his position and immediately verified that he was in fact bitten. After verifying this, medical personnel began to monitor the individual's vital signs to ensure that no side effects were experienced from the bite. However, there were side effects! About thirty minutes after being bitten the individual began to feel lightheaded and the bite began to swell. Upon noticing this First Officer Lead gave the command for everyone to put their headgear back on. However, his command was seconds too late. The mosquitos had covered the man in seconds. The only part of him that was still able to be seen was the soles of his space suit boots. Unlike common mosquitos experienced on earth though, these mosquitos were not just a nuisance, but could drain a person's blood within seconds. Seeing the swarm attacking the man in this manner, First Officer Lead immediately gave the command for military personnel intervene and attempt to secure him and everyone else to board the Eclipse Voyager.

Now back aboard the Eclipse Voyager, the remaining landing party scurried to kill what was left of the mosquitos on the man's body. After all of the mosquitos were killed one of the medical personnel placed one of the dead specimens in a vile, so that it could be later studied. Other medical personnel rushed to do everything in their power to revive the lifeless man. However, all attempts were unsuccessful. Now contacting Eclipse 8, First Officer Lead informed the captain of the events that had taken place. Captain Owens then responded, "Proper protocol will be followed. Upon entrance into the Eclipse 8 landing bay, all members of your party will report to the medical holding bays for decontamination. After decontamination procedures are completed, the deceased personnel is to be examined, as well as, the specimens collected."

After decontamination procedures were complete First Officer Lead accompanied Captain Owens to the bridge of Eclipse 8, where he back briefed the captain on all events that took place. After the back brief was complete Captain Owens then called Chief Medical Officer Green and instructed him to conduct an autopsy of the deceased member to see why he was the only one attacked on the planet's surface, and what the possible causes of death were. Following this Chief Medical Officer Green was to conduct a dissection of the mosquito to see what knowledge could be gained on the newly encountered species.

After several hours of studying the deceased male's body and the mosquito from A1's surface Chief Medical Officer Green believed that he may have found the reason that the man had been attacked. However, the only way to know for sure was to test his theory. To do that however they would have to return to A1's surface. He believed that the male had been attacked due to increased levels of iron in his blood. The man's iron levels were higher than the rest of the individuals that took part in the landing party. It was Chief Medical Officer Green's opinion that the mosquito could smell the iron in the man's body and that is what led them to him. However, the actual cause of death was the venom that the mosquitos injected before pulling blood from the individual. The venom that was injected was so potent that it not only contaminated the individuals blood supply, but also caused the man's heart to stop beating. Almost like the man had been given ten shots of adrenaline at one time.

Chapter 13
Testing a Theory

Because of the current situation Captain Owens did not want to send another landing party to A1's surface. Instead, he felt that it was best to contact L.I.G.H.T. and the Deep Space Station Command to gather their input on the situation. He knew that current events would raise some concern though, as Eclipse 8 had only been on mission for just over a month and the death took place on their first exploration. Regardless Captain Owens knew that his decision was the right one.

As soon as Captain Owens came to this decision, he told First Officer Lead to summon the Deep Space Station on the ships communication interface system. First Officer Lead in a fury of moves quickly brought the interface system up, and all stood by patiently until the Deep Space Station Command appeared on the screen. However, the Deep Space Station Command did not wait for Captain Owens to speak. Instead, President Hays immediately came over the interface and said, "Captain Owens I am gathering that the first exploration mission has been completed. What news of success do you have for us?"

Captain Owens remained silent for a few moments after this comment, and then he replied, "Sir we have good news; however, we also have bad news. I will lead with the good news and then follow with the bad. First off, our landing party successfully landed on the surface of A1. While on the surface they were able to gather over 2,000 samples of minerals and raw materials. They were also able to gather over 100 new species of vegetative life. However, around the ten-hour mark on their mission they experienced not only a casualty, but a death among the crew."

Immediately President Hays cut Captain Owens off and said, "What do you mean there was a death? Was it due to equipment error? Or was there a threat on the planet's surface?"

Captain Owens then stated, "Sir, this is actually the reason that I am contacting you. At this point in time, I am seeking your advice. Sir the individual that was killed was one of our military personnel. However, the manner in which he was killed was not a situation that has ever been encountered."

President Hays then said, "Okay, Captain Owens you have my attention at this point. We knew that this mission would be difficult and casualties were possible. Explain the situation to me, and we will go from there."

Captain Owens then replied, "Sir while on the planet's surface intelligence gathered that the planet's air was safe to breath. So that in mind, after a majority of the specimens had been gathered to be studied, the landing party took off their suit headgear. While their headgear was removed medical personnel monitored their vital signs, as per regulation. However, one of the military personnel was bitten by a mosquito. At first this, this did not seem to be an eyebrow raising occurrence, as we knew that there could be some life among the planets that we were set to explore. However, shortly after the individual was bitten, he began experiencing symptoms of light headedness and swelling at the bite area. Upon the individual experiencing these symptoms First Officer Lead went to give the command to don their helmets, but it was too late. While he was trying to give this command the individual that had been bitten was swarmed by mosquitos. In turn, leading to his death. While boarding the Eclipse Voyager however a mosquito specimen was able to be collected."

Now knowing what led up to the death of the crew member President Hays then asked, "Okay so what do we know about the specimen at this point? Also, was there any contributing factors that could have led to this occurrence?"

Captain Owens at this point said, "Sir at this point I will hand you over to our Chief Medical Officer so he can better explain the situation."

Shortly after this, Chief Medical Officer Green stepped up to the command interface and said, "It is good to see you sir, however, I wish it would have been under better circumstances. What we know at this point is that the military male had increased levels of iron in his blood. Probably due to a poor diet. However, it is my belief that this is why the mosquito bit him. No other member of the landing party showed increased iron levels. Also, upon testing the mosquito specimen the blood contained in the specimen was high in iron. This was not the overall cause of death though. The cause of death was a form of venom that the mosquitos injected before drawing blood from their victims. The venom that they injected was almost like a form of super adrenaline. When the military male was swarmed, he was injected with so much venom it caused heart failure."

President Hays now deep in thought then responded, "So how do we know that it was an increased iron level that caused these mosquitos to bite only the one member of the landing party? Could there be other additional factors?"

Chief Medical Officer Green immediately replied, "Sir it is my belief that if the mosquito would have been after any form of blood or any blood type, multiple members of the landing party would have been bitten. The specimen collected had the highest levels of iron in his body I have ever seen. I believe that the iron keeps the venom that the mosquitos have in their body at a tolerable level. To answer your second question, Sir there is no way of knowing if there were other contributing factors. For all I know, he could have provoked the mosquito; in turn, causing him to be swarmed and bitten. But I believe that it is in our best interest to test the theory. If I am right, we will be able to continue to collect the specimens that we need from the planet, and it will aid in identifying preventative measures that should be taken in the future so instances like this one do not occur again."

Upon finishing President Hays called Captain Owens back up to the command interface and said, "Captain Owens I am sorry for the loss of one of your crew members. However, I believe Chief Medical Officer Green is correct. We need to gather as much information on each planet as possible. After we conclude this discussion get with the medical team and see if they can come up with a safe way of testing this theory without endangering any further crew members. If the manner that you come up with is feasible then continue the exploration. If the theory that Chief Medical Officer Green has come up with is wrong, cease operations on A1's surface and move to your next objective. Once these actions have been completed summon us on the command interface system again and let us know what the results are."

Captain Owens immediately acknowledged President Hays' comments and closed down the interface system. Upon doing so he looked at First Officer Lead and said, "Accompany me to the medical bay. Let's see what Chief Medical Officer Green has up his sleeve." Shortly afterwards the two men arrived at the medical bay where they were greeted by Green.

Green immediately began the conversation by saying, "Okay, so here I have three vials of blood. One vial has an increased level of iron in it. The other two vials do not. To test my theory one vial with normal readings will be shot out of the Eclipse Voyager. The impact will cause the vile to burst. If nothing is drawn to the broken vile, then the second specimen will be shot from the Voyager. The second specimen shot from the Voyager should be the specimen with the increased iron levels. If mosquitos are drawn to this specimen, then we know it is in fact that the mosquitos are drawn to increased iron levels. To confirm this theory, the third vial will be shot from the Voyager. Again, if nothing is drawn to that vial the theory will be proven. However, all members of the landing crew will have their blood tested this time before leaving. I do recommend that even if we find out this was the cause of the attack that crew members leave their headgear on though. I don't like to chance fate."

Captain Owens happy with this resolution, immediately gave the command for the landing party to have their blood tested and re-board the Eclipse Voyager. Hours afterward, the Eclipse Voyager once again landed on A1's surface. Upon arrival, First Officer Lead gave the command to eject the first vial from the craft. After the vial was ejected the crew waited for one hour but saw no mosquitos in sight. Seeing that there was no reaction First Officer Lead then gave the command to eject the second vial. However, this time seconds after the vial busted it was swarmed by mosquitos. Seeing that there was an immediate response First Officer Lead then told personnel to eject the third vial while the mosquitos were still present. However, the busted vial had no effect on the mosquitos and they did not move to its location.

At this point it was safe to say that Chief Medical Officer Green's theory was correct. After the mosquitos cleared the area the landing party once again exited the craft. After exiting the craft, the crew spent several hours once again collecting samples from the planet's surface. Picking up where they had previously left off before the incident. The crew while collecting samples this time even found various types of fruit and vegetables that had been overlooked previously, as they blended into the plants that they grew on. However, the specimens would have to be tested before it could be safe to assume that they were edible. If they posed no threat they would be added to the countless number of fruits and vegetables that were already being grown among Eclipse 8's atrium. A mission that initially looked like it would be a failure had quickly turned into a success. Now as night approached the crew gathered their last samples and made their way back to the Eclipse Voyager.

Once the Eclipse Voyager arrived at Eclipse 8 the landing party once again sat through the twelve-hour decontamination period. However, this time the mission had been a success. Seeing that the mission had been a success Captain Owens contacted L.I.G.H.T. and Deep Space Command and informed them of the results and the success of Chief Medical Officer Green's theory.

Chapter 14
The First Encounter

Several months had passed since the exploration of A1 and Eclipse 8 was now making its way to D9. As it was the next closest planet that proved to be promising in terms of resources and the possibility of being inhabited. Up to this point all members of Eclipse 8 remained motivated as their mission so far and exploration to the surface of A1 led to the discovery of 427 minerals and elements that could be used to substitute those that had been depleted on earth. It was also found that some of the substances could be used among the ship. One primary example of this was uritanium. Uritanium looked almost like a metallic rock. Research found that the uritanium was an efficient fuel source and lasted longer than the current source used on Eclipse 8. Also, many of the fruit and vegetable samples collected proved safe to eat. Although majority of the samples gathered were destroyed while undergoing research some seeds were able to be salvaged from the plants. Among those seeds was a plant that was named the heroshifruit. This fruit looked much like a banana; however, it was orange in color and tasted like a pineapple when eaten. Unlike a banana, the peel of the fruit could also be eaten and proved to be very high in calcium and potassium. Mr. Red despite having only received about ten seeds was able to grow countless numbers of plants from these seeds. He grew so much, in fact, that it became one of the favorites that were served in the mess hall or galley.

There was even a use found for the venom that the mosquito possessed. After extensive research scientists found that the venom possessed by the mosquito could be diluted and injected into injury sites. When administered to a wound in small quantities the venom helped to speed up the recovery process. The venom also proved to be useful if mixed into the fertilizer used within the atrium. When mixed with the fertilizer the venom caused plants to mature 10% faster than had been experienced in the past.

All seemed to be going well this far in the mission as failures were reversed and turned into success, and Eclipse 8 experienced positive feedback from Deep Space Command. Until all of the sudden a tiny dot was seen on the ships tracking system. As soon as this dot appeared the operator summoned Captain Owens from his quarters. Once at the ships bridge Captain Owens made his way to the operator and asked, "What do you have for me?"

The operator immediately responded, "Sir, I don't know if we have a reason to be alarmed or if there is an error with my system, but I have picked up a lifeform within the bounds of our tracking system."

Captain Owens then said, "At this point it is too far away to be able to identify what it is. However, I will report the occurrence to Deep Space Command if the lifeform gets any closer."

Several days had passed since the lifeform had shown up on the ships tracking system. However, the lifeform seemed to stay the same distance from the ship. Until it mysteriously vanished off the edge of the tracking system. However, it did not vanish for long! About six hours after the lifeform vanished off of the edge of the tracking system it appeared again right in front of Eclipse 8. As soon as this happened Captain Owens was called to the ships bridge. Confused on how the object got so close to Eclipse 8 without being seen on the tracking system, Captain Owens ordered everyone to man their stations.

Afterwards, he then ordered the bridge's visor be lifted and the defense shield raised. However, when the visor was raised there was nothing to be seen. Captain Owens furious at this point told operators to run checks on all systems to ensure that they were properly working. However, they were to keep the ships defensive shield up for safety. Minutes later operators reported to Captain Owens that system checks had been conducted and no errors were present.

Upon hearing this Captain Owens then attempted to contact Deep Space Command to inform them of their current situation. However, when trying to establish communication the ships interface command was shut down. At first crew members felt that this was due to a glitch in the ships operation system or electrical error that occurred while rebooting the system. To fix this error engineers worked tirelessly to restart electrical systems again. However, all attempts were unsuccessful. Until suddenly a ship appeared in front of them. The ship was much larger than the Eclipse 8, and looked much like what researchers had seen before the mission had taken place but refused to identify.

Now knowing that there were actually alien lifeforms present in the Galaxy they were currently in Captain Owens ordered bridge personnel to do whatever they could to establish contact. However, since the command interface system was down secondary measures would have to be taken. At first communication was attempted through a series of flashing lights. When this failed to work, the bridge personnel attempted to send a series of sound waves through space and deflect them off of the other ship. Still there was no response.

Now almost out of ideas, Captain Owens stood staring at this ship but said nothing. At this point he did not feel that a defensive altercation should take place as they hadn't even made contact yet. Seeing that communication was not going to be able to be established Captain Owens then came up with another idea. Instead of fighting or establishing communication Eclipse 8 would flee and avoid a negative confrontation until they were able to figure out another method of contacting the ship.

With this plan in mind Captain Owens contacted all personnel among Eclipse 8 using the intercom system and said, "At this point in time we have established that there are other forms of life in this solar system. We currently have a foreign or unidentifiable ship directly to our twelve o'clock. Despite continued efforts we have been unsuccessful in establishing communication with them, and are unsure if they are hostile. Because we are unaware of what weapons capabilities the other ship has and do not wish to start an interstellar war, or cause an avoidable incident, we are going to employ defensive strategies and attempt to lose the ship or flee until such a point that we are able to establish some form of communication with them or receive guidance from L.I.G.H.T command. I do ask that all personnel brace yourselves though as we are unsure if deploying these measures will lead to an attack."

As soon as Captain Owens finished his transmission, he looked at First Officer Lead and said, "On my command I want the ships thrusters full to the rear and the ships cloaking mechanism engaged. When we get far enough away from the ship, I want thrusters engaged full to the front at a direction of thirty-two degrees. Hopefully this will allow us to pass by them and get to a point where we can once again attempt to establish communication with them or L.I.G.H.T. and Deep Space Command."

Minutes later Captain Owens loudly commanded, "Thruster's rear and cloak engaged." The ship moved quickly backwards almost throwing its occupants to the ground. Seconds later Captain Owens commanded, "Full forward!" The ship almost at the speed of light now started to pass the much larger ship, while being invisible to the naked eye. However, it was not invisible to the larger ship. About the time Eclipse 8 was going to pass the larger ship it stopped dead in its tracks, losing all power. Everyone among the ship was in a panicked state at this point. However, before anyone could make a rash decision the ships command interface began to flicker until all at once it revealed a matrix of numbers on the screen. Although no one could understand the mass amount of numbers, all knew that it was some sort of message.

It was several minutes after the numbers began to continuously run across the interface that Captain Owens looked at his First Officer and said, "Get all personnel up here that understand coding and anyone else that thinks they can decode this message." First Officer Lead unhesitant immediately moved from level to level among ship gathering up all personnel that he thought could decode the message. Once at the bridge Captain Owens showed each the interface and asked if any could make sense of what the series of numbers meant. The message repeating the sequence:

2.5.23.1.18.5_20.8.5_16.15.18.1.12_15.6_20.9.13.5_1.14.4_19.16.1.3.5_

6.15.18_8.5_23.8.15_16.1.19.19.5.19_20.8.18.15.21.7.8_20.8.5_16.15.18.20.1.12_

13.1.25_14.5.22.5.18_18.5.20.21.18.14

Hours passed and still no one was any closer to deciphering the message. When all of the sudden the ships power slowly flickered back on. All confused by the events that had just taken place everyone began to scurry to restart their systems. However, once all systems were back up and operational to everyone's surprise the message was gone, as well as, the ship that temporarily held them captive.

Not knowing at this point if the ship would be back or was still monitoring them. Captain Owens made the decision to continue movement away from the area and to get to a position that helped protect them from further attacks. At this point he knew he needed to report the intelligent life to higher and regain communication with L.I.G.H.T. and Deep Space Command.

Hours later, after countless attempts, Captain Owens was finally able to establish communications with L.I.G.H.T. and Deep Space Command. Upon the communication being received, Captain Owens stated, "President Hays, L.I.G.H.T., and Deep Space Command, we have made our first contact with another intelligent lifeform. However, an effective means of communication was not established. The other beings did send us a message and we are continuing to work diligently to decipher. What we do know from the encounter at this point is that the lifeform has technology far more advanced than anything we have seen, and was able to render us helpless in seconds. No hostile threat or intent was received, and at this point I feel that it would be in the best interest of L.I.G.H.T. to continue mission, and try to continue to establish communications if we have further encounters. Once the message has been deciphered, we will report back to you and inform you of the message content. What are your thoughts on the matter President Hays?"

President Hays was all but surprised at this point in time, as he had been made aware before the mission took place that there was a possibility of other lifeforms in the galaxy that they were exploring. However, due to the nature of the incident he replied, "I applaud you for not causing an undue conflict. I ask that you do exactly as you say and continue to try and un-code or decipher the message and report back to us its contents. However, I ask that you do not seek out the lifeform. If the lifeform wants to make further contact, I am sure that they will find you, as they have previously done. I fear that if we pursue the lifeform, it may cause them to feel that we are threatening them. At this point continue to your set destination of D9. Once there conduct operations according to plans and report back to us. If further contact is made, I ask that you report back to us as you have done now. Are there any questions Captain?"

Captain Owens at this point told President Hays that there were no more questions and assured him that operations would continue, upon which point he shut down the interface. Afterwards Captain Owens told all members of the bridge that if anymore lifeforms appeared on the tracker he was to be notified immediately, and evasive measures would be taken. He then ordered them to replot their current course and continue on to D9 as planned. After he was done giving the bridge instructions, he then addressed the rest of the ship, "Ladies and Gentlemen of Eclipse 8, we have just had our first encounter with another intelligent lifeform. Although it did not go according to plans, it did not end in disaster. That being said, if further contact is made, we will make you aware immediately and do our best to ensure that you remain safe. While at the same time trying to establish a peaceful relationship. Operations are to resume as normal. Bridge, out!"

Chapter 15
Intelligent Life at
a Cost

Eclipse 8 had now been on their current mission for nine months. However, they had not accomplished as much as they had hoped to up to this point, due to the amount of time that it took to travel from one planet's location to another, and other outside factors such as the individual that was killed on A1 and intelligent life that took the crew by surprise. The research that had been conducted up to this point had proved to be well worth the sacrifices that had been made though. Now at D9 the crew prepared to conduct research on the new planet's surface. However, while running scans on the planet's surface prior to departing Eclipse 8 the crew found that there were lifeforms among the planet. Although they could not tell what the lifeforms were, they could see them moving about the surface.

This not only sparked curiosity but also put crew members on high alert as previous encounters had not gone according to plans. Captain Owens not wanting to lose another crew member this time decided that not only would he accompany this landing party, but he would also include more military personnel than he did previously. Captain Owens felt that the increased presence would deter any attacks. This increased presence would also increase their odds of survival if an attack was to happen.

Now aboard the Eclipse Voyager all members sat quietly as they made their way to the planet's surface. Though all were eager and full of anticipation to see what lurked about the planet, many had thoughts of what they may encounter. Once on the surface Captain Owens instructed personnel to conduct operations as they had before. First running scans to see where lifeforms were in respect to their current position. That is, if there were in fact lifeforms. They also took this precaution to ensure that the immediate area on the planet's surface was stable enough for operations to continue. Once these scans were complete an environmental scan was run. When results were processed it was found this time that the atmosphere had the same oxygen content as Earth. This in mind, Captain Owens gave everyone the command to take their helmet off before departing the craft. Captain Owens felt that this may help reduce the intimidation factor if there was life in the immediate area.

After everyone had removed their headgear Captain Owens then gave the command to lower the crafts ramp. The ramp slowly came to a stop on the planet's surface revealing a landscape much different than any the crew had seen. The trees on the planet's surface seemed unreal. They were black in color and reached almost two hundred feet in height. The leaves protruding from them were a bright orange in color. Almost as if they were trapping the sun's rays inside them, as they too were emitting light. The leaves draped from where they sprouted on the trees and went all the way to the planet's surface. There was no grass or vegetation, but instead an orange sand substance that sparkled in the light. Also, the landing party could not immediately see water, but could hear it in the distance.

All members of the crew eagerly collected samples around the Voyager for several hours before one member looked at the captain and said, "I think I heard movement in the distance." Upon the crew member telling the captain this he ordered military personnel to look around the area.

Shortly after giving this command one of the military personnel returned to the captain and said, "Sir there is something over here that you need to see." Captain Owens, hearing this, immediately made his way to the place where the individual had come from. To his surprise when he got there, he saw several footprints. Although they were not normal footprints. The footprints that they had found were much larger than a normal man's footprint and there were only three toe prints.

Captain Owens curious at this point called back to Eclipse 8. Upon reaching Eclipse 8 and First Officer Lead he stated, "We are going to break protocol a little bit here. We have found signs of life on the planet's surface. At this point we are going to leave a small party to secure the Voyager and make our way further into the tree line and see if we can find indigenous lifeforms. If a hostile threat is encountered, we will make our way back to the Voyager and return to Eclipse 8."

Upon finishing his statement First Officer Lead responded, "Sir protocol does not allow you to move over 1,000 meters from the Voyager unless a second party deploys to the surface and secures the Voyagers landing site." At this point Captain Owens being the impatient man that he was shut off his radio.

He then looked at the landing party and said, "I guess there are some communication problems. Let's split up, the individuals identified will remain with the Voyager, while the rest of us see if we can find what left these footprints."

All members of the crew just as eager as the captain complied with his orders and slowly made their way into the forest. As they walked, minutes seemed like hours, and hours seemed like an eternity. Although no other lifeforms had been found.

The crew was about ten miles from the Voyager when they once again heard a rustling noise in the trees and to their surprise saw a man. However, he was unlike any they had ever encountered before. The man that they had come across was much taller than any of those among the crew and was as orange as the leaves on the trees. Once the lifeform realized he had been spotted though he immediately took off running. As soon as the military members saw this, they immediately began chasing him while continuously yelling "STOP, HALT." Captain Owens, in turn, told the military personnel to stay in place, however, none listened to his command.

Moments later what was left of the landing party broke through the tree line to see the military personnel being held captive with their own weapons. Captain Owens at this point yelled, "Stop, we didn't come here to harm any of you. Despite what you may think we want peace!"

Upon hearing this one of the men with a black headdress on, that had been fashioned from bark from one of the trees, yelled, "Put down your weapons!"

All members of the landing party at this time were shocked. They did not expect the individual to speak in English. The members of the man's tribe were just as surprised as the landing party as they were ready to kill the men that were chasing them.

Now everyone was at a standstill. No one said a word but you could feel the tension in the air. To break the silence Captain Owens then said, "We can take you to our ship and feed you, or give you things that you need."

The leader of the tribe immediately responded, "We will not leave Olaria, but you can accompany us to our village, where we can feast and discuss peace."

Captain Owens ecstatic replied, "Let me call my ship and let them know that we are okay, so that they don't send more unneeded soldiers." The leader simply shook his head yes to acknowledge the captain.

Afterwards the captain and the local tribe leader moved only a few hundred meters away from where they currently were to find a village high in the trees above the planet's floor. A river ran through the village that was so clear it almost looked as if it was part of the ground. Also, to the landing parties surprise villagers did not greet them in haste, but were happy to see their presence. Once the leader had reached his home, he sat the landing party down. He then introduced himself as Salaron, leader of the people, and gave the landing party a brief history of his people and how they came to be.

Afterwards he asked the captain why they had come to his planet. Captain Owens almost embarrassed then explained that his people used their planets resources in haste when they were young. He then continued to explain that they were now seeking out new planets. Planets where resources could be gathered to replenish those that were necessary for survival so that earths people could continue to exist. In closing he also explained that they were looking create or make treaties with other lifeforms so that they could not only help themselves, but help others.

Salaron then said, "My people have all that we need. We are the most intelligent form of being in this universe. If you would like I can give you and your people, this knowledge as well."

Captain Owens was puzzled at Salaron's comment and asked, "How have you come to be the most intelligent lifeform?"

Salaron then stated, "The river of life gives us the ability to see into the future. Which in turn, let's us determine what our fate will be. Sometimes this knowledge is a blessing. Other times it proves to be a curse. It allowed us to know when and where you would be arriving. That is the reason you were able to learn of our existence. We allowed you to find us. We had seen countless times the future that would come to be. It was also through these premonitions that we learned how to approach this encounter so that life was not lost. To demonstrate this, we will now give this knowledge to one of our finest warriors. So that you may see how it works."

Moments later the warrior entered the room. At first, he did not seem to be intelligent at all. However, all of that changed in a matter of moments. After the warrior entered the room Salaron's wife brought in an object wrapped in the leaves of one of the trees. To everyone's surprise when it was unwrapped it was a small clay pot almost the size of a shot glass. Upon unwrapping it, the warrior knelt in front of Salaron. Salaron then placed the small clay pot in the warriors' hand, at which time he drank the contents. Moments later the warrior hit the ground and started shaking. As soon as this happened the medical personnel on the landing party jumped to their feet and rushed to the man's side. However, Salaron stopped them and said, "Wait, in moments his life will be forever changed." Seconds later the man awoke on the ground and rose to his feet.

Once on his feet, he looked at Captain Owens, and said, "I know the reason that you are here and I would like to accompany you on your travels, as long as, it is okay with my leader."

Captain Owens in shock at this point responded, "If it is okay with Salaron, I will accept you as part of the crew. I will also swear my allegiance to help your people if they are ever in a time of need."

The Warrior then responded, "My name is Alazana, and Captain Owens we will soon never be able to return here. I know this presents many questions for you, but they will all be answered in time." Captain Owens confused at this point accepted the man's proposal.

Afterwards medical personnel asked Salaron if the water had any lasting effects on those that drank it. Salaron then stated, "Once the life force has entered your body and has bestowed knowledge upon you, you have 30 years of life remaining. However, I have learned that it is a small price to pay for the knowledge of the future. My time now is coming to an end, but the knowledge that I have will never die, instead it will be passed on to another when my body is placed into the ground and once again returns to the river." Continuing, he then said, "It is time now that I escort you to your ship. Alazana will accompany you and answer a question that you have been seeking the answer too."

At this point Salaron escorted the men the long distance back to their ship. Once at the ship all men bid their farewells to each other. Once everyone had boarded the ship the tribe that had once stood outside the door had vanished almost as if they had never been there. Although everyone on the landing party knew that they had due to their new crewmember. Upon closing the ramp Captain Owens called up to Eclipse 8 and informed them of their return and the added member of their team.

Chapter 16
Questions Answered

After everyone was back aboard Eclipse 8 many questions still remained. Maybe more so than had been present before the landing party had landed on D9, which was now known as Olaria. However, the main question on Captain Owens mind was, what did Alazana know the answer too? Before Captain Owens could even ask him though, Alazana looked at Captain Owens and said, "You seek the knowledge that I have. Although I am hesitant to give it to you. I don't wish to anger my new friends and colleagues."

Captain Owens then said, "Alazana what do you have the answer too? I will not hold you responsible for the information you provide me with, but I need to know."

Alazana at this point looked at the captain and said, "I have an unwanted answer to a question that you have. However, the answer will not set your mind at ease. Instead, the answer will cause chaos among your crew and leave you searching for another answer."

Captain Owens then replied, "Just tell me the answer that you have, and even if it does cause chaos, once the dust settles we can look for the next answer together."

Alazana pleased with what the captain said responded, "You encountered another being before us and they left you a message. A message that you could not decipher."

Captain Owens now looking at Alazana surprised said, "Yes, it is just a sequence of numbers that we have not been able to make any sense out of."

Alazana now smiling said, "You sought the answer too hard. The answer is very clear if you are not looking for it. The numbers given correlate with a specific letter in your alphabet. They were not attempting to harm you when they made contact, but instead were trying to warn you. That being said, the message that you received says, Beware the portal of time and space. For he who passes through the portal may never return."

Captain Owens now confused responded with, "What do you mean may never return?"

Alazana then said, "If I were to base my answer purely on logic, I would interpret it to mean that the space time continuum varies each time you pass through it. The probability that you will go back to your original point of entry is highly unlikely. However, in some cases if the object passing through is small enough, such as the rovers your command sent through. Then they will be able to return to their original location. The rovers that did not return had a change in overall mass. They contained samples retrieved after initially passing through the black hole. Therefore, they were sent to a different galaxy or parallel universe. I believe the individuals you encountered knew this and were warning you that with the size of your ship you will continue to go to different galaxies with little likelihood of being able to return to your own galaxy."

At this point everyone on the bridge of Eclipse 8 was in a panic. Captain Owens in shock at this point said, "Alazana are you sure that is what the message said? If so, I need to contact L.I.G.H.T. and Deep Space Command. If we cannot return to our own galaxy and universe then this may be a pointless mission. None of the peace treaties and trade agreements will make a difference if we can't send things back to L.I.G.H.T. and Deep Space Command. Not to mention it would mean we are doomed to travel space for eternity with no hope of returning home. A fate that in turn could lead to our death."

Alazana then replied, "Captain I am certain my translation is correct. However, your treaties and trade agreements are not being made in vane. You are not only forging agreements, but making allies or better yet friends. Ones that can assist in the continued survival of those you have been placed in command of. Also, the inability to return and death is not certain! If you find the right passage, then success is possible. However, if you fail to find this passage then you must determine your own fate."

Captain Owens now staring at Alazana asked, "Where do we find this passage or know if it is the correct one?"

Alazana however only answered, "I cannot see past this galaxy. However, other galaxies may hold the answer to your problem."

At the end of the conversation Captain Owens was somewhat discouraged, but knew that he had to maintain his composure so that others among the crew did not lose hope. Also, as much as he hated to admit it, he knew that Alazana was correct and that their endeavors were not pointless. Despite these facts Captain Owens knew that he still had to

112

contact L.I.G.H.T. and Deep Space Command. This in mind, he looked at First Officer Lead and said, "Bring up the interface!"

Once the interface was up President Hays asked, "So do we have any good news this time."

At which time Captain Owens flopped into his command seat and replied, "Sir the mission on D9 or Olaria was a success. We have now added a new member to our crew and forged a peace treaty. However, we now have a new problem."

Hearing this President Hays responded, "That is great news. Also, you said a new member of the crew? You encountered another being that was capable of communicating with you. With news as good as what you just gave me how could there possibly be any bad news?"

Hesitant Captain Owens then responded, "Well, Sir, the message has been deciphered by our new crew member. The message reads, Beware the portal of time and space. For he who passes through the portal may never return."

After hearing this, President Hays sat for several minutes before responding, "What do you mean he who passes through the portal may never return?"

Captain Owens now looking at Alazana then turned and said, "The ship is too big to pass back through the black hole and return to you. According to Alazana if we pass through the black hole we will end up in another galaxy. His explanation makes perfect sense and explains the initial rovers and equipment you were never able to retrieve. I would stake my life and my crew's life on what he has told me. Sir, the only way of knowing for certain though is to try it. If we end up back at Deep Space Command, we will know that the message was false information. However, if we don't end up there, we know we need to start looking for an alternate way home, which I also regret to inform you does not exist in the Galaxy we are in."

President Hays was now at a loss for words. However, after a few moments responded, "Captain Owens, as much as I don't want to abandon the mission at hand. You have completed many of the tasks that you were charged with. So, if you come back now, the mission will not have been a total failure. I give you permission to attempt to pass back through the black hole and return to our location. However, if you attempt to pass back through the black hole and are lost to yet another galaxy, know that the distance might be too great for us to be able to communicate with you. In the event that this happens your new mission will be to gather intelligence and data from the different galaxies as previously planned. However, while you do this, your new primary mission will be to return to the Deep Space Station. Are there any questions at this point Captain?"

Captain Owens with no questions shook his head in acknowledgement and replied, "Sir, we will make our way back to the black hole and our initial point of entry immediately. The trip will take a couple of months though. Once there we will attempt to pass through the black hole and back to the Deep Space Station and command. We will contact you before attempting to pass through. That way you will know what happened if you are unable to raise us through communications efforts. If we are unsuccessful, we will turn the ship around and make one more attempt to pass through in hopes that it at least brings us back to our current location. If both attempts are unsuccessful, we will continue to seek out new black holes in hopes that one leads us home, while continuing with our current mission to find new inhabitable planets and resources." Upon finishing his comments Captain Owens shut down the command interface and told First Officer Lead to plot a new course to their original entrance point.

Now complete with their two-month return trip Eclipse 8 sat once again staring into the void that they had once passed through. Although unlike the first time there was not as much knowledge on where it would actually take them. Before entering this time though Captain Owens came over the ships intercom system and said, "Ladies and Gentlemen of Eclipse 8, we are once again about to attempt to pass through the black hole that led us to this galaxy. I hope that it takes us back to our loved ones and Deep Space Command. However, if recent knowledge that was bestowed on us proves to be true, it will not. That in mind, I ask you brace yourself and pray to whatever God you pray to for assistance. Bridge, out!"

After his announcement Captain Owens looked at First Officer Lead and said, "Take us in Officer Lead." At which point First Officer Lead put the ships thrusters to full ahead and they once more went into the darkness.

Chapter 17
Uncharted Territory

While passing through the black hole, the journey once again seemed to take longer than it actually did. Many felt that this was simply due to the anticipation of what would happen when they entered the void or arrived on the other side. Where others felt like the passage through the black hole itself actually slowed down time. However, once on the other side it would seem like an eternity to all. Now complete with the journey Captain Owens looked at First Officer Lead and said, "Officer Lead try and raise L.I.G.H.T. and the Deep Space Station on the interface." First Officer Lead tried for several minutes; however, communication could not be established. Upon not being able to establish communication First Officer Lead looked at Captain Owens and said, "Multiple attempts have been made sir, but there is no signal present. We are unable to establish communication at this time." Captain Owens now sitting deep in thought then responded with, "Try all frequencies and channels. If you are still unable to reach them attempt digital messaging. If that fails hold our current position and begin mapping of the current solar systems and Galaxy."

After several hours and multiple failed attempts at raising anyone on the communication devices, personnel had finally completed the navigational charts. The charts this time though were completely different than any of the other galaxies or solar systems that they had been to. As when the charts were completed this time, it looked as if the solar systems were simply mirrored over and over again throughout the galaxy. No one galaxy varying from the other and no one planet showing differences among them.

Now realizing that communication with L.I.G.H.T. or anyone else for that matter would not be possible and not knowing if it would ever be able to be established again Captain Owens pulled First Officer Lead to the side and said, "Lead, I want you to get all of the ship's leaders and level commanders to the ships conference room at once. We have several issues that we need to discuss, and time may be of the essence." First Officer Lead immediately complied and called for all of the level commanders and other leadership to report to the conference room over the intercom system.

After about thirty minutes had past all leadership had made it to the conference room and sat quietly and patiently for Captain Owens arrival. All talking among themselves and bringing up the several questions they had for him. It was about this time that Captain Owens opened the conference room door. Upon his entry everyone became silent in anticipation of what he had to say and why he had brought them together. Although most of them felt they knew why the meeting had been called. Captain Owens now standing behind his chair began to speak, "Everyone I am sorry for the short notice and having to bring you all in like this. I am sure many of you will or do have questions for me at this point. I do ask that you hold all questions to the end of the meeting unless you are being directly asked a question by myself. Once we get to the end of this briefing, I will answer all questions that I am able to. Some of you may have questions that I simply don't have an answer for. If that is the case bare with me and we will try and find an answer together." After stating this Captain Owens moved his chair backwards and sat down, then pulled himself up to the tables edge.

Now sitting at the table with everyone, Captain Owens placed his notebook in front of him, and said, "Here is what we know this far. Communication is not able to be established with L.I.G.H.T. or Deep Space Command. On top of that, we are in an unknown galaxy to L.I.G.H.T. To add to this problem researchers believe we are not able to pass through a black hole and return to our previous destination. Which seems to be true, as when we passed back through black hole that led us to the last galaxy we conducted operations in, we did not end up at our starting point. On a more positive note, L.I.G.H.T. and Deep Space Command engineered this ship to last indefinitely without outside support. We also still have a surplus of supplies on the ship and a very qualified crew. Despite these things I like all of you would like to return back to deep space command, or at a minimum the previous galaxy that we came from. At least in the previous galaxy we had an ally. Here we are alone and unafraid. My fear at this point is that crew members will begin to panic. I ask that during this period you keep order among your levels and operational areas. What won't help our situation is widespread panic. If you are a leader ensure that all regulations and guidelines are followed. In turn, this will allow us to maintain our resources and order so that no further issues arise. It will also aid us in solving other problems that we may have. So, working our way around the table does anyone have any ideas at this point?"

Everyone sat at the table very quiet after the Commander made this statement. Captain Owens then pointed at the first man to his left. However, instead of replying he simply shook his head no and said, "I have no suggestions; however, I will ensure that anything you put out is enforced." Captain Owens then looked at the next man who also nodded his head no. It wasn't until the captain reached the sixth person that a comment was made.

The individual looked at the captain and asked, "What if we were to turn the ship around and pass back through the black hole again? Would it take us to another uncharted galaxy or would it take us to one that we have already charted and conducted exploration missions in?"

Captain Owens then looked at the man and replied, "If the black hole we just passed through did not take us back to L.I.G.H.T. and Deep Space Command there is no way of knowing if it will lead us back to the galaxy we just came from. However, that is an option that I have already thought of and is up for debate at this point. If passing back through the black hole gave us the slightest chance of going back to the previous galaxy, we would at least be able to regain communications with L.I.G.H.T. Command. Worst case scenario we end up in another uncharted galaxy and still have no form of communication with L.I.G.H.T." After finishing with this Captain Owens took notes of the option. He then moved on around the room.

Several individuals later another individual finally spoke, "And if that takes us to another galaxy what are the options then."

Captain Owens with a sigh replied, "Anything from here on out is new. It is situations that have never been experienced before. However, if it takes us to another uncharted galaxy then we make the best of a bad situation and continue with the previous L.I.G.H.T. and Deep Space Command guidance. We will continue to look for resources that can be used on Earth and try and forge treaties throughout the different galaxies which we pass through. If the right individuals are encountered, then maybe they can give us the answer or knowledge that we need to return. If not, then hopefully personnel among the ship can find the answers."

After going around the room and hearing everyone's input and ideas Captain Owens felt the best option was to attempt to pass back through the black hole in hopes that it would take them to their previous destination. However, Captain Owens felt that it was a decision that should be made by all and not just him. As they all had just as much at stake as he did. That being said, Captain Owens asked one of the men at the table if he could borrow his hat. The man looked at him in confusion and then handed it to him. After receiving the hat Captain Owens stood up and said, "This is not a democracy and I feel that everyone should have the right to vote on this decision. That being said, we will all vote and then place our votes in the hat as it is passed around. At the end we will tally up all of the votes and the decision with the most votes will be the chosen path." Everyone simply shook their head and agreed as they started getting pieces of paper out.

About 15 minutes later, all votes had been cast and the hat had made it all the way around the room. Once it was back in Captain Owens' hands, he turned the hat upside down. He then started placing the votes under the category in which they fell. After separating the votes, it was clear that almost all personnel in the room felt the same way that he did. All but a select few had voted it best to attempt to once again pass back through the black hole. That being the case, Captain Owens stood up and said, "Well it is final, we will turn the ship around immediately and attempt to once again pass through the black hole. If it does not take us to L.I.G.H.T. and the Deep Space Station or the galaxy that we just came from we will continue with the L.I.G.H.T. and Deep Space Station's Mission and try and forge treaties with other intelligent life, as well as, try and find resources that can help humanity."

As soon as Captain Owens finished with his statement, he released all personnel back to their perspective levels and departments. Upon exiting he told all leadership to ensure that personnel that served under them were also made aware of the situation, and that he too would address the crew as soon as he made it to the bridge. Upon reaching the bridge Captain Owens looked at First Officer Lead and said, "Turn us around, Lead, let's give this one more shot." First Officer Lead then immediately turned the ship around. While turning the ship around Captain Owens came over the intercom and said, "Crew of Eclipse 8, as you have been informed or are being informed now we are currently in an uncharted galaxy and have no means of communication with L.I.G.H.T. or the Deep Space Station. To correct this issue, we are going to once again pass through the black hole in hopes that this issue can be resolved. If, however the issue is not resolved we will continue on our current mission until a time that it is. At this time though I ask you to once again brace yourselves and prepare for entry into the darkness." Captain Owens then closed out the transmission and looked at First Officer Lead and said, "Back to the darkness from which we came." Immediately First Officer Lead put the ships thrusters to full and Eclipse 8 once again disappeared.

Chapter 18
The Mission Continues and an Enemy Is Made

Eclipse 8 had once again came to a slow halt outside of the black hole. Upon stopping all levels reported up their status. At which point Captain Owens looked at First Officer Lead and said, "Lead, pull up the navigational charts and see if the current galaxy can be found within the archives. If it cannot start the navigational charting process based off of distance to each planet this time and not just resources. Also begin a search of lifeforms within the immediate area."

He then turned around in his chair and looked at one of the other bridge operators and said, "Try and bring up L.I.G.H.T. or the Deep Space Station on the command interface. If they can't be reached immediately try changing to different frequencies to see if that helps."

About an hour after searching through the navigational chart archives First Officer Lead turned to the captain and said, "Captain we are in another uncharted galaxy. However, if other navigational charts are correct, we are parallel to a galaxy that has been charted. As the constellations and planets on the edge of this galaxy reflect on two other charts."

Captain Owens immediately responded, "At least there is a glimpse of hope this time. Lead I want you to begin the navigational charting process as I told you too. Once that has been completed let me know and chart a course to our next destination."

Upon finishing with First Officer Lead, Captain Owens turned to the individual that he had trying to establish communication and said, "Have you had any luck in establishing communication with L.I.G.H.T. or the Deep Space Station?"

The individual quickly responded, "No Sir we have not been able to establish communication with them or anyone else for that matter."

Captain Owens surprisingly then commented, "Switch all frequencies back to their set position and continue to monitor in case someone does try to raise us on the interface."

Afterword's Captain Owens once again came over the ships intercom and said, "Crew of Eclipse 8 we have once again found ourselves in an uncharted galaxy, and unable to establish a means of communication with L.I.G.H.T. or the Deep Space Station. However, there is some hope as the galaxy that we have found ourselves in this time reflects partially on other archived charts. I ask that you keep morale high as we continue to search for a solution. For the time being though we will continue with our mission and attempt to find new lifeforms and civilizations to form treaties with, as well as, resources that can help mankind. Operations will continue as planned. That is all, Bridge out!"

After finishing with his comments, Captain Owens looked back at First Officer Lead and said, "Lead take us to the first destination on the chart."

Lead then looked at Captain Owens and said, "Sir we are estimated to be there within three weeks, although at this time it does not look like there will be any resources there that will be beneficial to us."

Three weeks later Eclipse 8 arrived at the charted planet. One that the members of the crew had come to know as the Blue Dragon planet. As the clouds or atmosphere of the planet looked to be made out of fire but had streaks of blue running through it at the same time. Once at the planet, the captain had a different planning idea in mind. In order to mitigate casualties on the planet's surface, this time a probe would be shot into the planet's atmosphere and continue on until it logged the entire planet's surface. The probe would allow the crew to get readings of different elements that made up the atmosphere, as well as, show if any lifeforms were detected on the planet's surface. If no threats were revealed, then a landing party would be sent to gather specimens and samples as before, if they could.

About twelve hours after the probe was shot into the atmosphere of the planet, Eclipse 8 began to receive the readings that they had been so anxiously awaiting. It looked as though the atmosphere was made up of a number of different things. However, it was primarily made up of Nitrogen, Phosphorus, and Helium. All elements that could be withstood by the suits that the landing party would be fitted with. However, these elements would not allow the landing party to breath naturally. Instead, they would have to use the suits breathing systems. This would also cause the

125

landing party to remain in their full suits during their entire expedition. Which, in some cases, would hinder their mobility. Upon looking farther into the results received it looked as if the surface of the planet was made entirely of hardened lava or igneous rock. The planet showed no forms of vegetation or lifeforms. However, the landing party would have to be on the planet's surface to ensure this.

After reviewing all of the results Captain Owens moved to the Eclipse Voyager where he was greeted by the rest of the individuals that were set to go on the landing party. Once all were present, they boarded the Voyager and began their descent to the planet's surface. Unlike the previous planets that the landing parties had been on, the crew this time would have to find a spot to land the craft where it would be free from harm and easily accessible. As there were still parts of the planet's surface where molten lava continued to flow through cracks. After almost an hour of circling the proposed landing site the crew finally found a place where the craft could safely land.

Seconds later the Voyager gently sat down on the planet's surface. Once on the surface Captain Owens gave military personnel the order to exit the craft and secure the area. After the area was secure the rest of the personnel exited as well. Immediately all personnel began gathering what little samples they could find. However, this time resources were limited and it looked as if not many samples would be found.

About two hours after being on the ground Eclipse 8 showed another lifeform approaching the ship. Upon seeing this First Officer Lead immediately contacted Captain Owens and informed him of the situation. Captain Owens knowing that they were not complete with operations however, told Lead to try and establish communication with the approaching lifeform, and that he was going to continue on his current expedition. He then informed Lead that if any complications arose or the other lifeform proved to be a threat to contact him again and they would conclude their operations.

Lead tried for several hours reaching what proved to be a ship later on. However, all efforts that he made ended in failure. It wasn't until the ship was about thirty minutes from Eclipse 8's position that Alazana turned to Lead and said, "The approaching beings are not friendly, you should summon the captain immediately and request his presence."

Lead somewhat confused looked at Alazana and replied, "What do you mean they are not friendly? We have not even been able to establish communication with them, and they have shown us no hostile intent." Seconds later Alazana grabbed First Officer Lead and touched his forehead to First Officer Leads. Upon touching foreheads First Officer Lead immediately became incognizant of everything that was going on around him and Alazana began transferring images into Leads head. Images of an attack. After transferring the images to First Officer Lead he then pushed himself away and dropped to the floor. Lead now seeing what Alazana was talking about immediately called Captain Owens and said, "Sir the lifeform we spotted is a ship, and if Alazana is correct this ship is an imminent threat." Captain Owens upon hearing this immediately ordered the landing party to load the Voyager and quickly took off from the planet's surface.

Once in-flight Captain Owens called back First Officer Lead and said, "How do we know that this ship is a threat?"

Lead then replied, "I don't know how to explain it. Alazana grabbed me and transferred images that he saw into my head allowing me to see them. I didn't have time to ask about the images more in detail though."

Captain Owens then responded, "What do you mean that you didn't have time to ask about the images. Give me Alazana, I want to speak with him!"

Seconds later in a weary voice Lead responded, "Captain he is indisposed of at the moment. Transferring the images to me caused him to collapse. He is currently on the medical level receiving care. However, they informed me that he will make a full recovery."

Captain Owens replied, "Well if Alazana was that confident in his visions then raise the ships defenses immediately."

Moments later the Voyager landed in Eclipse 8's docking bay. Unlike usual though Captain Owens did not remain in the holding facility. Instead, he quickly made his way to the bridge. Upon entering the bridge, a burst of fire was fired from the other ship striking Eclipse 8. However, the advanced shield that had been placed on the ship absorbed the blast. Immediately following a second and third blast was received. Captain Owens realizing that there was no avoiding the situation gave the order to return fire. Although it seemed as if the blast had no effect on the other ship either. Immediately following Eclipse 8's counter-fire the opposing ship fired a series of shots once again at Eclipse 8. This time however, it showed that the ships defense shield was weakened. Captain Owens seeing this ordered that power from the lower levels, as well as, the shots received be redirected to the defensive shield to bring it back up to maximum capability. He then ordered Weapons Specialist Gauge to increase the power of the shots being fired to 150%. Moments later Gauge acknowledged the captain and said, "Prepare for shots Captain." At which time Eclipse 8 fired a shot that not only crippled the opposing ship, but momentarily seemed to render it lifeless.

Now at a standstill everyone was unsure of what to do. However, just when Captain Owens was about to give more commands the ships interface system came on to show a being that was black in color and to his surprise had no eyes. Although its head was glowing, revealing veins throughout the being's body. At first it didn't seem like the being was going to speak. However, to everyone's surprise it already was. The being was communicating with Captain Owens telepathically. Captain Owens first asked the being, "Why have you shown hostile force? We are peaceful beings." However, the being did not respond. Instead, the being put pictures of previous wars fought on Earth in the captain's mind. Captain Owens upon seeing the images then said, "That was previous battles that no longer rage. We are now a peaceful race. Is there any way that we can come to an agreement or truce so that this type of encounter does not happen again in the future?

However, the being once again entered the captains mind and said, "There will be no peace until the entire human race has been eradicated. This is the will of my superior." After receiving this message, the captain once again went back to his normal functions. Upon gaining control of his body again the enemy ship quickly flew away and Captain Owens gave the command to move on to the next location and immediately retired to his quarters before being questioned.

Chapter 19
The Mission Must Go On

Hours after the encounter Captain Owens remained in his quarters. Troubled by his disappearance First Officer Lead made his way to where the captain resided. Upon reaching the captain's quarters First Officer Lead knocked on his door hesitantly.

Captain Owens responded, "Whatever it is, it can wait. I will be back to the bridge within the hour."

First Officer Lead then replied, "Captain Owens I would like to speak with you if it is not an inconvenience." Captain Owens at this point made his way to his quarters door and hit the open button causing the door to slide out of the way revealing First Officer Lead. To his surprise First Officer Lead stood there with a bottle of aged Jack Daniels in hand.

Upon entering the captain's quarters, First Officer Lead asked Captain Owens for two glasses. Captain Owens then reached in a small cabinet above his kitchen counter top and placed the glasses on the counter, he then asked Lead what he had come there for. First Officer Lead however simply smiled and said, "I think we should have a few drinks and then we can talk about that." Now about a half way through the bottle, both men had clearly forgotten the encounter that they had just experienced. However, Lead had not forgotten the reason that he was there. It was at this time that First Officer Lead began to address the captain.

"Captain Owens, I know that these are troubling times for you. As you were made aware of the dangers that could be present before we left. Despite this we still went forward into the unknown. We knew that no crew had ever been faced with these situations and that we may not be able to return. However, we must put these things behind us and continue to move forward. As if we do not move forward, we are not helping ourselves or mankind. That being said, this is one of those situations that must be put behind us. You cannot dwell on these occurrences, if you do you will not be doing anyone any good."

Captain Owens at this point sat speechless for several minutes before responding, "I think all of us may have gotten in over our heads. We thought we knew what we were getting into and troubles that we may face, but really, we were oblivious as to what was ahead."

First Officer Lead then nodded his head and said, "Captain, many years ago when I joined the L.I.G.H.T. academy, I had no idea what I was getting myself into. My father who was also a Captain tried to keep me far away from the L.I.G.H.T. academy. However, he passed away in a training accident many years ago. I wanted to know exactly what happened, and what he was doing that was so important. After many years of searching for an answer, I found that the search itself for the knowledge was pointless. The answer that I was looking for was irrelevant. We all have paths that we must take, and although there may be obstacles that stand in the way, it is our responsibility to continue on our own path and overcome those obstacles."

Captain Owens at this point simply nodded and then replied, "Lead the obstacles in our path may in turn equal death. An obstacle that I myself am prepared for. However, I am not ready to take that risk with other people's lives and the ship. How do you lead an expedition of uncertainty?"

First Officer Lead then looked at the captain and said, "Captain, I believe you simply lead confidently, and through that confidence you gain the loyalty of those around you. Though it may take time, if you continue to do what we all know you can, then anyone and everyone on this ship will follow you to whatever fate has in store. Whether that fate be death or returning to the galaxy that we came from."

Captain Owens at this point had a look on his face that First Officer Lead had never seen before. The look was that of confidence. Shortly afterwards Captain Owens looked at First Officer Lead and said, "The mission must go on."

First Officer Lead then said, "Yes, Captain, and it is through your leadership that we will prevail."

Captain Owens then looked at Lead and said, "It has been a long time since I have had a friend, But Lead I now see you as a friend. I want to thank you for coming here this evening and re-instilling a since of pride within myself. First thing in the morning we will re-evaluate the mission, make changes where we see necessary, and then brief the crew. However, I feel we should both be sober for that so that we don't make any hasty decisions right away." First Officer Lead shook his head and agreed with the captain, then exited his quarters.

The next morning, First Officer Lead came to find Captain Owens waiting outside his door with coffee as he exited to move to the bridge. Captain Owens immediately said, "I know you were headed to the bridge, but I feel that this morning is a good morning to walk about the ship and visit the various levels and get to know our crew on a more personal level and find out how they are doing and if they have any needs that are not being met."

First Officer Lead then responded, "Okay, Captain, I am at your disposal." The first stop that the two men made was at the medical level. Once at the medical level the two men met with Chief Medical Officer Green.

Upon meeting with Green, Green said, "To what do I owe the honor gentlemen?"

Captain Owens then said, "Well, Mr. Green, we figured that we would go throughout the ship today and see how operations are going and if anything is needed by level leadership. Is there anything that we can do for you Mr. Green?"

Chief Medical Officer Green at that point looked around and said, "As far as supplies and equipment we are good. We also have an excellent facility; however, we are very shorthanded when it comes to staff. Is there anything that can be done about that?"

Captain Owens then looked at First Officer Lead and said, "Officer Lead when we reach the bridge, I want you to look at the ships manning and pull anyone that is not filling an important role and have them placed under Mr. Green's leadership. Even if they have no background in the medical field, I am sure that training can be conducted by Mr. Green that will leave them fit for duty in this area. Does that work for you Mr. Green?"

Chief Medical Officer Green shook his head yes and then said, "Captain, I thank you. It is hard to conduct operations when you are shorthanded. We had trouble just the other day when Alazana collapsed. With two of my staff on the landing party it left only myself and two technicians here on the ship manning the medical facility. The help you offer me now will allow us to conduct operations in a more fluent manner. Also allowing us to give medical treatment in a timelier manner."

After leaving the medical level it was time to visit the ships atrium. The two men walked for about ten minutes before reaching this area. However, upon their arrival they saw no one. The two men curious at this point walked around the atrium for several minutes yelling for Mr. Red but got no response. After about twenty minutes of searching the atrium, they finally found Mr. Red in the laboratory at the back of the atrium where he sat at a microscope. Upon entering Mr. Red looked up from the microscope and said, "I was wondering when you would find your way here."

Captain Owens at this point said, "Mr. Red how are operations going here in the heart of the ship? Are operations going the way that you would like or are there changes that need to be made?"

Mr. Red sat for a minute and then responded, "Well, Captain, as you can see, we are limited for space at the moment. Growth at this point is phenomenal. On top of that, the new species of plants that we have brought in, have managed to cross bread with other plants. In turn, this has created new fruits that are able to be consumed. At this point, I would have to say no there are no changes that need to be made. However, while conducting exploration missions on planets I do ask that you try and find soil that will be able to be transported to the ship so that the current soil can be switched out. I feel that the current soil will only have enough nutrients to sustain about ten more cycles of growth. Although that may seem like a long time it is never too early to get a jump start on a future problem."

Captain Owens again looking at First Officer Lead then said, "First Officer Lead I want you to get with Mr. Red later and find out exactly what he is looking for in terms of soil. Once we have that information, we will do our best to facilitate his request." Upon finishing this statement First Officer Lead acknowledged and then the men shook hands with Red and exited the atrium.

With two levels down there were only two left to visit, as the other areas of the ship were common areas and living quarters. The next area that the two men made their way to was the weapons and defense level. Upon entering the level, the two men were immediately greeted by Weapon Specialist Gauge. Gauge immediately looked at the two men and said, "I am glad you are here Captain Owens I have some proposed changes to make to the ships weapon system and the defense system as well."

Captain Owens shocked by the greeting looked at Gauge and said, "By all means go ahead sir. Especially if it will benefit us."

Gauge then said, "Our encounter the other day led me to a discovery that I had not noticed originally. When the ships lasers are fired it drops the ships shield momentarily.

This means that we are most vulnerable when we fire. However, I have found a way to prevent this. By redirecting the power from the ship's thrusters to the defensive shield we will be able to keep the shield up in situations such as the one we were faced with yesterday. The other proposed change is that when firing the ships weapon system, we do so in shorter bursts at a higher power or frequency. When we absorbed the shots fired the other day it almost fried the electrical system down here because we were holding too much power. However, if we fire shorter bursts at a higher frequency, it will cause more damage and will also keep the ships electrical system from being overloaded."

Captain Owens now nodding in a pleasant manner looked at Gauge and said, "Well is there anything you need from us?"

Gauge paused for a moment and then said, "Really Sir the only thing I need is your permission to make these changes. Other than that, everything is going excellent here."

Captain Owens looked at Gauge and then said, "Gauge, I authorize the proposed changes. On top of that I would also like you to look at the Voyager and see if there is any way that you can put a defensive shield on the ship, as well as, fit it with some sort of weapon system? I hope it is never needed, but it is better to be safe than sorry. Also, if you have any changes, you feel need to be made in the future do not hesitate to find me and let me know."

Gauge then shook the two men's hand and said, "No problem, sir, and I will be sure to find you when I have ideas in the future."

The two men now made their way to the last level of the ship, the engine level. Unlike most of the other levels, when entering the engine level there were people everywhere working on pieces of equipment and conducting checks. The two men knew that they would have a hard time finding Sun Tu through all of the chaos that was taking place so they immediately asked one of the crew members where he was. The individual did not say anything though, instead they simply pointed across the level. Once at the other side of the level the two men had still not located Sun Tu. So, they once again asked another individual, who to their surprise was exactly who they were looking for. Sun Tu simply looked at the two men and said, "Operations are going flawlessly. The new fuel source provided burns cleaner than previous fuel sources and allows us to reach higher speeds when the thrusters are engaged. The only down side to operations right now is we received slight damages in the attack yesterday that we are now working to fix."

Captain Owens with a troubled look on his face then said, "Will systems be fully functional within the week?"

Sun Tu laughing then said, "Sir, they will be within the day."

Captain Owens then looked at Sun Tu and said, "Thank you Sun and do not hesitate to let me know if you need anything." At this point Sun Tu simply bowed and went back to work.

Now having made it to every level the two men made their way back to the bridge. Upon entering the bridge, the men felt better about operations and both knew that they had to continue on. Captain Owens now with a new sense of livelihood looked at one of the crew members of the bridge and said, "Intercom please."

As soon as the intercom was up Captain Owens said, "Crew of Eclipse 8, today I have made my way around the ship and have seen the excellent jobs that all of you are doing. I have also made notes on what I can do to help you. I will ensure that whatever changes or requests you have given me are taken care of in a timely manner. Despite previous occurrences the mission must continue. We are not only on another mission, but are serving as a line of hope to those we love and care about at home. That being said, we will continue our current mission, and we will eventually return to L.I.G.H.T. and Deep Space Command. Maybe not today, maybe not tomorrow, but through our hard work and dedication we will once again be with those that we love. Bridge Out!"

Chapter 20
C4 – The Abandoned Planet

Moments after the captain had made his announcement, he looked at First Officer Lead and said, "I feel we should start looking at planets within the immediate area which look promising for exploration missions. Maybe we can find a new civilization with which treaties can be arranged. Then again maybe we can solve the soil issue that was brought up by Mr. Red." First Officer Lead as usual simply acknowledged what the captain said and then started conversing with other members of the bridge.

About four hours later First Officer Lead approached the captain and said, "Sir I believe we have found the next planet to conduct missions on. However, if scans prove to be accurate there looks to be no life forms inhabiting the planet. It looks to be inhabited only by plant life."

Hearing this the captain sat for a moment and then said, "Well maybe we will not be able to form a treaty, but we may be able to solve our soil issue. I want you to go down and inform Mr. Red that he will be accompanying the landing party this time. I as well, will be accompanying the landing party. That means while I am away you are in control of the ship Mr. Lead." First Officer Lead acknowledged the captain and then immediately left the bridge to go inform Mr. Red.

As soon as First Officer Lead left the captain looked at the bridge crew and one of his second officers (which at this point all looked like a deer in the headlights) and said, "2nd Officer Langley I must step away from the bridge for a moment as well. In mine and First Officer Leads absence you will be in charge. However, if there are any issues call myself and First Officer Lead back up to the bridge immediately."

At this point the 2nd Officer was in shock. He looked at the captain and in a stuttering voice said, "R-r-r-o-g-e-r Captain." The captain now laughing stepped through the bridge doors and continued walking down the corridor.

First Officer Lead, was now at the atrium. Once entering the atrium, he easily found Mr. Red unlike the last time that he and the captain went looking for him. Mr. Red was walking around the atrium testing the PH levels in the water that ran throughout nourishing the plants. As First Officer Lead approached the man this time though, he was startled as Mr. Red without seeing him, quickly turned and yelled, "Helllooooo, Officer Lead."

Surprised First Officer Lead jumped backwards. Mr. Red amused by his reaction then began laughing.

First Officer Lead then said, "Sir what was that? I am pretty sure you just took about three years off of my life."

Mr. Red still laughing replied, "Officer Lead you need to loosen up a little bit. I was simply messing around a bit. I heard the bay doors open upon your entry. What can I do for you this time sir?"

First Officer Lead shaking his head then said, "We are going to be sending an exploration team out shortly to conduct operations on C4. There seem to be no intelligent lifeforms inhabiting the planet. However, there is plant life. That being said, the captain would like you to accompany the landing part to see if the soil on the planet's surface will be suitable to bring to the ship to solve our current soil problem."

Mr. Red now smiling said, "I would be more than happy to accompany the landing party sir. Getting out of here for a minute might do me some good."

First Officer Lead then replied, "The captain or myself will notify you when it is time to move to the Voyager." Upon finishing his statement First Officer Lead turned and quickly exited the atrium to make his way back up to the bridge.

Captain Owens was now at the weapons level. Upon entering the level Captain Owens walked around talking to only crew members of the level at first to find out how they were doing. After talking to about ten members of the crew Captain Owens however knew that it was time to get down to business. Upon finishing his conversation with a crew member, he asked the individual where Weapons Specialist Gauge was. The crew member then laughed and said, "He is behind you Sir, He has been there for quite some time now." Startled, Captain Owens spun around quickly. Weapons Specialist Gauge however just looked at the captain as he stood there holding a big wrench.

The captain then said, "Why didn't you say something and what is the wrench for?"

Gauge laughed and said, "Well I was screening what my crew said. If they said the wrong thing, I was going to wrap this around their head."

Gauge Seeing the almost fearful look on the captain's face, then stopped laughing and said, "I am just kidding, sir. No reason to be worried. I actually just got done modifying the Voyager. A simple change to some of the wiring on the ship allowed me to add a defensive shield. However, you should know that it will not be able to sustain a blast like Eclipse 8 took the other day. The shield will simply only stop smaller less concentrated blasts."

Captain Owens in shock said, "Wow that was fast. However, I have to ask one more favor of you. Can the Voyager be modified slightly to allow for soil to be transported in it?"

Gauge then said, "Well, sir, I knew eventually we would have to haul something with the voyager. I didn't know if it would be additional personnel or something that we wanted to bring back to the ship. Because of that I have created a trailer that can be hauled by the Voyager. However, it will not be ready for about two to three more days."

Captain Owens then replied, "Okay Gauge, I want your primary focus to be that trailer until it is complete. Once you are complete with it and it is ready to be tested in operations let me know. I plan on using it during our next planet exploration. However, the next operation will be at a standstill until you are ready."

Gauge then looked at the captain and said, "Well I will put a rush on it. However, there is no way it will be finished within the next 24 hours. It will take that long to ensure that its operating systems are electrically and mechanically sound."

The captain then simply said, "I have the utmost faith in you sir. I leave this in your hands. Just call me when you have completed the project." The captain then shook the man's hand and exited the defense level.

Two days later the captain finally received a call from Gauge stating that the trailer was ready for operations. Upon receiving the call, the captain came over the ships intercom system and said, "All members of Eclipse 8 that are to accompany the landing party please report to the Voyager in one hour so that we can suit up and embark on our next exploration mission." All members that were on the landing party to include the captain then made their way to the Voyager. Once at the Voyager all personnel put on their suits and started conducting the checks that they were responsible for.

About three hours into mission preparation and hearing that all systems were a go the captain grabbed the intercom microphone on the Voyager and said, "First Officer Lead, if you would be so kind as to open the exterior doors, we are ready to embark on our exploration mission." Seconds later the exterior doors opened and the Voyager slowly exited the much larger craft.

The Voyager touched down on the planet's surface about 45 minutes after exiting Eclipse 8, and as they did with all missions, they began to run scans of the planet's surface to ensure that nothing had been missed and the crew would not be in harm's way when they exited the aircraft. Once scans were complete the crew exited the Voyager. All ground party members scurried around frantically taking samples of plant life and raw materials among the planet's surface. Mr. Red, whose agenda at this point was the main focus continued to pull the needed soil samples while at the same time running them through multiple tests to ensure that they would be suitable for crops. After several samples were taken, he finally found soil samples that were more than suitable. Upon this discovery all members of the ground party shifted their primary focus and began to collect soil and place it in the trailer that was attached to the voyager. However, the process proved to be very lengthy. In all, the process took about twelve hours. After the twelve hour operation however, the trailer was still not full. It was at this point that members of the ground party were so tired they could not continue to conduct operations.

Knowing that they had not completed everything they needed to, the captain came to a hard decision. Would they leave the surface of the planet and return the next day? Or would they inhabit the planet for the night, rest for a short period, and then continue operations again once everyone was rested. The captain with this in mind, pulled all members of the landing party back aboard the Voyager. Once aboard the Voyager he looked at everyone and held a vote to determine the next course of action. To his surprise though, all members of the ground crew wanted to stay in place and continue operations. He figured that this was probably mostly because they knew they would not be able to leave the landing bay due to decontamination procedures. However, was pleased with the decision as all crew members took turns sleeping throughout the night and running continuous scans. When morning came the last person to stand guard woke everyone up, so that operations could be continued. Once resumed one of the lower ranking personnel summoned the captain to the front of the Voyager and said, "Sir, this may be nothing, but when I was conducting scans last night of the area, I lowered the intensity of the scans and found what looks to be buildings not far from this location."

The captain surprised said, "Show me, Son." Quickly the individual conducted the same procedure that he had before. About ten minutes into the scan, he froze the screen that he was looking at.

He then said, "Sir, if you look at these lines on the screen, they are not normal or natural terrain features. They look more like some type of structure. I may be wrong and it could simply be fatigue, but if I am right, then someone has been here before, or they still are." Upon hearing this new information, the captain's curiosity was sparked.

The captain then looked at the crew members and said, "As we did before, we will put exploration of the possible buildings to a vote. However, not all personnel will accompany us to the location, if it is voted that we conduct a reconnaissance. A majority of personnel will remain here and finish operations. This will also allow for a faster exit if it is so needed." The crew once again came to a final decision. They would move to the location of the possible buildings to see if life did in fact exist on the planet. Once this agreement was reached the captain pulled four military personnel from the landing crew and began to move to the possible building location.

About an hour after embarking on their journey to the buildings all members of the party began to realize that life did or at one point had existed on the planet as they began to see smaller structures as they approached the location they had seen while conducting scans. The ground party now only about two miles from the location saw the edge of the tree line beginning to fade away. As they reached the edge of the tree line all members stood in shock. Although they saw no life forms, they did see some of the most magnificent buildings and structures any of them had ever seen. The structures and buildings were all built into the side of a mountain face.

At the edge of the city on both sides stood two magnificent statues that looked to be some sort of alien lifeforms. They were carved out of what looked to be a black marble like substance. The detail in each statue being more intricate than anything seen before. The buildings spanned the length of the mountain face. Each having very prominent features with walkways leading to them. No one structure looking like the other. In the center of the city there was one structure that looked to be much larger than the rest with spiraling columns along the front, each with what looked to be a different lifeform among the top of them.

Surprised by the structures and startled at the same time Captain Owens instructed all members of his party to remain hidden from sight for a long period of time. Captain Owens felt that this was the best course of action so that they could monitor the structures to see if any alien lifeforms could be spotted. However, as time passed, they realized that there was no one inhabiting the structures. After this conclusion was reached Captain Owens gave the command for his ground party to approach the structure. However, as a precaution he had the Voyager crew, who were now finished with their operations, load back up into their ship. Captain Owens also had Eclipse 8 focus their weapon systems on that point on the planet's surface.

Slowly the crew approached the structures until they were standing at the great columns. To their surprise they were not greeted by anyone though. They stood there in complete silence. Not even a noise from a distant animal could be heard. Captain Owens at this point said, "Well I guess there is only one way to find out if anyone is here, and that is knock and see if anyone answers." Captain Owens after saying this pounded on the door four times. However, to his surprise on the fourth knock the door slowly creeped open. Hesitant on entering Captain Owens prepared the military personnel and told them that they would enter first. All members acknowledged and stacked up one behind the other beside the door. Then after a waiving motion from the first man they rushed inside. However, no shots were heard. Instead, all anyone could hear over their intercoms were the sounds of amazement that each man made.

Seconds later Captain Owens himself went inside the structure and to his surprise there were statues scattered about within the structure and beautiful carvings covering the walls. However, there was no one in sight and the plants that filled vases laid lifeless.

The only thing that Captain Owens could think is why would anyone abandon these beautiful structures. The crew members looked through all of the structures for hours. However, no sign of struggle or force could be seen anywhere. They could not find any reason for someone to leave this place. As it was almost night though the crew knew that they could not stay another night. They did not have enough provisions on the Voyager to sustain them. It was because of this Captain Owens called the Voyager and had them move to their location.

Once at their location one of the members of the crew gave the suggestion that they should take some of the relics and if they encountered another intelligent life form, they could ask about them. They also felt that maybe Alazana could provide some insight. Captain Owens agreed and began to load some of the smaller statues up into the Voyager along with some of the smaller paintings that were on the walls. Now having completed their operation, they closed the back door to the Voyager and began their trip back to Eclipse 8.

After the decontamination period was complete the crew moved the statues to an empty room among the ship's cabins. A room that was to be deemed the relic room and set up much like a museum by the captain. After all statues had been moved the captain brought Alazana to the room to ask him about the relics. However, all Alazana could tell him was that they were from an ancient race, and he had never seen anything like them.

Although no answers were able to be reached in terms of the relics the crew was successful in their mission overall. As the soil that they had taken from the planet's surface would allow for several more cycles of plant growth on Eclipse 8. Which was more important at this moment than forming a treaty or finding another intelligent lifeform. Knowing that they couldn't dwell on their findings the captain knew that they had to continue on, if they hoped to find answers or a way back to their own galaxy. Captain Owens at this point looked at First Officer Lead and said,

"Thrusters and engines full ahead, head toward the darkness of space to see what the next passing planets have in store."

Chapter 21
Second Encounters
and an Alliance

Many days had passed since the crew conducted their exploration on C4, and still they traveled without a new target planet in sight. However, they did have one in mind. A planet that if scans proved to be accurate held multiple life forms. What those lifeforms were however, remained a mystery. The target planet in question the crew had come to call E5 or the blue planet. As from a distance it looked as if the planet was entirely covered in water. Which also raised questions on if the lifeforms that were being picked up were intelligent or simply some form of aquatic vertebrae. Regardless the planet was the closest that proved to be promising within the galaxy in which they traveled. A galaxy that would soon become named the Gemini galaxy.

After about a week of travel Eclipse 8 neared the planet which they planned on conducting operations. Like the many missions before the crew that would accompany the landing party was identified by the captain. However, this time the captain told First Officer Lead he would accompany the landing party while he remained aboard the ship. The captain also stated that First Officer Lead was to land on whatever landmass he could find. If a landmass was not able to be found once near the surface, he was to do a water landing and remain in place to see if contact could be established with the lifeforms in question or if they could at least be identified.

After two more days Eclipse 8 had reached the Blue Planet. It was now time to conduct exploration operations. All members that were part of the landing party boarded the Voyager and conducted pre-mission checks as they normally did. Then the Voyager like so many times before exited Eclipse 8. As the crew neared the surface no landmasses could be spotted. First Officer Lead because of this had the Voyager hover above the water surface for several minutes before calling back to the captain and informing him that a water landing would have to be conducted. Not surprised by this Captain Owens simply said, "As we discussed before no one will exit the craft once the water landing has been conducted. Instead, you will remain aboard the Voyager and attempt to make contact with the alien lifeforms in whatever way you can or at least identify what we are picking up. If, however, you cannot establish a clear line of communication within an eight-hour time period you will return to Eclipse 8. Is that understood?"

First Officer Lead at this point simply responded, "Yes, Captain, I acknowledge all and will comply."

Moments later communication between the Voyager and Eclipse 8 stopped and the Voyager focused on trying to establish communication with the lifeforms in question. At first the crew attempted to use the loudspeaker that the Voyager had been fitted with by broadcasting a simple message. However, after hours attempting this method, no contact had been made. Next the crew attempted to establish communication by a series of taps almost like Morris's code which not only sent vibrations through the water but sound waves throughout the atmosphere. However, still no communication could be established. About five hours into the mission one of the crew members suggested that the Voyager simply send out a constant vibration through the water in hopes that whatever was occupying the planet would be annoyed.

This went on for about two hours and still yielded no results. The crew about ready to give up suddenly felt the Voyager jolt sideways. At this point First Officer Lead said, "Start the engines and put them full thrust up." In a series of movements, the pilot of the craft started the Voyager. However, when he went to thrust upwards the Voyager didn't go anywhere instead it stayed in place. Moments afterwards the ship actually began to lower. At this point the crew were all fearful that they would drown on the small ship. However, to their surprise after the Voyager went down about ten feet the water around them began to disappear. To everyone's surprise they were not only under the water but they were in a chamber.

Confused and unsure on what was taking place, First Officer Lead immediately told the military personnel to prepare for engagement. Military personnel hearing this immediately placed a magazine in their weapon and chambered a round. It was at this time the crew could see through the ships windows that they were surrounded by a series of tunnels. Moments later the Voyager came to a stop and the chamber turned slowly until the rear of the craft was facing a tunnel that was much larger than the rest.

First Officer Lead unable to reach Eclipse 8 now knew that he had to make a decision on what the crew was to do. Knowing this he ordered that the ramp be lowered and the military personnel exit the ship and clear the immediate area. As soon as the ramp was lowered however the weapons were ripped from the military personnel's hands and sucked to the walls of the chamber that they were in. One of the crew members immediately ran to the wall and attempted to free his weapon several times, however remained unsuccessful. It was obvious at this point that the chamber had been magnetized.

Seconds later the door to the larger tunnel slid open to reveal a being that looked much like the statues aboard the voyager. However, the being had gills running from the edge of his ear all the way down to the collar of his shirt and his nose was much smaller and almost flat. Members of the Voyager crew at this time were terrified and remained backed against their ship. However, to their surprise the being began to speak. While the being spoke, everyone simply looked at him confused as none of them had heard a dialect like the one, he used.

The being at this point realized that none of the crew could understand him. Knowing this he simply signaled for the crew to follow him. However, no one person moved from their position. All members of the crew at this point simply stood still in fear for their life. Moments later, however, First Officer Lead looked at his crew and said, "If we stay here, we are dead. We can't get out of the chamber we were lowered in. We should go ahead and follow him.

Worst case scenario is that we die but if we stay here, we are dead anyway." The crew not happy with this decision but knowing he was right followed First Officer Lead and the strange being down the large corridor.

Each member walked quietly behind one another unsure on what fate had in store for them. Each having different thoughts run through their minds. Some had thoughts of being killed as soon as they reached their destination. Others feared that the odd being had plans to eat them. Some simply felt if the being wanted to harm them, he would have right away, and that they were being taken to someone that could understand them.

Regardless the crew continued to follow the being. After several minutes the crew and the being reached another door. Once there, the being signaled the crew to remain in place, which they did. The being then stepped forward to the door and a series of green lights started sweeping around his body. Once the lights stopped a red laser projected from the center of the door and scanned the individual's eye and the door then slid open. As soon as this happened the being looked at the crew once again and signaled them to follow him. However, this time when the crew stepped through the door, they found themselves in what looked to be an operation center. Individuals that looked just like the being they were following frantically raced around the room and pointed at positions on the large monitors scattered about. Shortly after entering the room another one of the beings much larger than the one that the crew had been following approached the crew. He then began to speak to the much smaller individual. Seconds later the larger of the two looked at First Officer Lead and said, "By looking at you I gather that you are a humanoid, and if my education serves me correctly this is the dialect that you are most comfortable with." First Officer Lead simply nodded his head in disbelief.

After overcoming the initial shock First Officer Lead then asked, "Who are you and why have we been taken prisoner?"

The being simply looked at him chuckled and then said, "Sir, I am Vlandamire and we have not taken you prisoner, but instead brought you here to keep you safe."

First Officer Lead confused at this point then said, "Safe from what?"

Vlandamire then said, "There is a being approaching our planet that kills any lifeform they encounter. They are a predator species that simply travel about the galaxy and take whatever they can so that they can continue to exist."

First Officer Lead now starting to panic looked at Vlandamire and said, "We have a ship full of personnel just outside of your atmosphere and if that is true, they are all in danger."

Vlandamire then said, "If you can promise me that your people will not become hostile, I will allow you to contact them. However, if you in any way feel that they will become a threat to my people it will not be permitted. Furthermore, if they become hostile at any point throughout communication they will be eliminated."

First Officer Lead looked at Vlandamire at this point and said, "To eliminate any possibility of hostility will you allow me to be the one to establish communication?" Vlandamire simply shook his head yes and moved to a control panel nearby.

Moments later Vlandamire hit a key on the control panel and a screen came up in front of First Officer Lead. As soon as the screen came up First Officer Lead could see the captain. Worried about their wellbeing the captain immediately said, "What is your location? Are you in any danger right now?"

First Officer Lead trying to calm the situation down said, "Sir we are below the planet's surface. The individuals we are with at this moment pose us no harm. They actually brought us to their location so that we were not in harm's way."

The captain confused at this point responded, "In harm's way from what?"

At that moment, Vlandamire stepped in front of the screen and said, "Sir at this point in time an enemy approaches our planet. An enemy that shows no mercy. I brought your personnel here to ensure their safety. If you assure me that you will pose my people no harm, I will do the same for you before this enemy arrives. Our planet has a defensive shield that will not allow the enemy ship to pass into our atmosphere once it is turned on."

Captain Owens at this point was skeptical until First Officer Lead said, "Sir if they wanted to kill us, they would have already done so. I feel that since these people know this enemy we should do as they say."

Captain Owens then responded, "Lead I will take your word. However, know at this point you are responsible for the wellbeing of every person aboard this ship. If this leads to our death you will be responsible."

First Officer Lead simply acknowledged what the captain had said and then Vlandamire said, "Captain, I will need you to lower your ship below our atmosphere. Once you are within our atmosphere look for a portion of the planet's surface that is glowing green in color."

Moments later Eclipse 8 was inside the planet's atmosphere. Once there, Captain Owens then said, "Okay we have identified the area that is glowing green in color. What do you want me to do now?"

Vlandamire then responded, "Simply land Captain and shut down your engines. Your first Officer and I will be there shortly to greet you. However, I will advise you to come unarmed. As if you bring any sort of weapon, we will take it as a hostile act and you will have to be eliminated." Captain Owens acknowledged Vlandamire even though he was uneasy about the meeting.

About five minutes, after the transmission Eclipse 8 came to a stop below the planet's surface. Captain Owens immediately exited the ship and stepped onto the very large platform that Eclipse 8 rested on. About the time that he stepped onto the platform a large door slid open and revealed First Officer Lead and Vlandamire. Surprised that First Officer Lead was okay Captain Owens moved forward to their location. Vlandamire at this point stuck out his hand which had webbed fingers as to shake the captain's hand. The captain still hesitant shook Vlandamire's hand and then Vlandamire said, "Sir if you will follow me, I will show you why we have taken these actions." Captain Owens simply nodded his head and followed the two men.

Once back in the operation center Vlandamire pulled the two over to a side room. As soon as all three were in the room the door slid shut and screens dropped down from the ceiling. As soon as the screens had reached their final positions images of the approaching ship were shown. However, to Captain Owen's and First Officer Lead's surprise this was not the first time that they had seen the ship. In fact, it was the same ship that had attacked them before.

Vlandamire could immediately tell that something was wrong once the two men saw the images of the ship. Seeing this he said, "By your reaction, I gather that you have seen this ship before?"

Captain Owens nodded his head and then said, "Earlier on in our voyage the same ship attacked us. The beings are black in color, have no eyes, and communicate telepathically. I thought they wouldn't be a threat anymore once we traveled far enough through the galaxy."

Vlandamire then responded, "Yes, Captain Owens, it is in fact the same beings. They are black in color because they absorb the souls of their enemies. However, there is not only one ship but several. The ship that you see now. The one that you encountered before is simply a scout ship. The mother ship is much larger and its weapon systems are far more advanced than the ones that your ship or even our planet is fitted with. That is why we have concealed ourselves below the planet's surface. If the beings do not see life, they will not waste their time with attacking or even exploring the planet."

Captain Owens then responded, "How then can this enemy be beaten or destroyed?"

Vlandamire in a sigh then said, "I do not know. The race known as the Soul Eaters have no home planet and have destroyed any and all races they have come in contact with besides ours. However, they almost wiped our race out

159

completely. It is only through hiding that we were able to survive."

At this point in time the ship was almost to the planet. Captain Owens a little worried at this point looked at Vlandamire and said, "What actions are you planning on taking right now?"

Vlandamire then said, "None, Captain Owens. Sometimes the best course of action is taking no action at all. If we do not attack the ship it will pass by and not even realize that this planet is inhabited or has lifeforms on it."

Captain Owens then said, "I hope you are right."

After about twenty minutes had passed to Captain Owens surprise the ship continued to pass by the planet. The three men simply watched until it was a safe distance away. Upon the ship passing Captain Owens looked at Vlandamire and said, "Sir, we are indebted to you. Is there anything that we can do to assist you?"

Vlandamire smiling then said, "Captain I ask only your friendship."

Captain Owens seeing this as an opportunity then said, "I can give you more than friendship. I would like to be your ally! If you ever need our assistance and we are in the area we will come to your aide." Vlandamire liked what the captain had to say and held his hand out once again as to shake the captains hand. This time though Captain Owens did not hesitate.

As the men exited the room Vlandamire looked at the two men and said, "Tonight to celebrate this new friendship we will have a feast. I would like for all of the members of your ship to be present if at all possible." Captain Owens then accepted his request.

Later on, that evening all members of the crew along with Vlandamire's people filled the dining hall of their great planet. All members who attended did so in great rejoice. Throughout the evening new friends were made and an alliance grew stronger. It was about two hours into the occasion that four of Vlandamire's military aged males came to Vlandamire and asked him if he would give his permission for them to accompany Captain Owens on his voyage. Vlandamire simply accepted their request.

Chapter 22
Mysteries Solved and New Courses Plotted

After the night had passed and it was determined that the enemy ship was far enough away that it no longer posed a threat it was time for Captain Owens and Eclipse 8 to depart Vlandamire's planet and continue on their journey. However, before leaving Vlandamire pulled Captain Owens to the side and said, "I know you long to return to your galaxy, and I hope that you somehow find a way to accomplish that feat. However, I hope that you keep a clear path to travel so that you can once again return. Hopefully the individuals that I have allowed to travel with you prove useful." The two men then simply shook hands and Captain Owens once again boarded Eclipse 8.

After boarding the ship Captain Owens made his way to the bridge, which was now already filled with its normal personnel. However, this time one of Vlandamire's men also filled a position on the bridge. The individual's name was Randalari. Randalari would assist personnel in terms of plotting new courses. Seeing that one of the new personnel was already filling a significant role Captain Owens simply smiled. Afterwards he came over the intercom and said, "If you would please start all operating systems and prepare to exit the blue planet." Randalari simply laughed when the captain said this.

Captain Owens now curious looked at the man and said, "Did I say something wrong?"

Randalari responded, "Sir, I did not mean to be disrespectful. The name of our planet is Celeriac. Which is part of the Gemini Galaxy."

Captain Owens hearing this then grabbed his chin and in a curious manner asked, "Why is it called the Gemini Galaxy?"

Randalari then pulled up a map of the galaxy and said, "If you look at all of the solar systems within this galaxy, many look like they are mirrored. However, that is not actually the case. If you were to visit some of them, they would not actually be physically present."

Captain Owens in shock now then said, "Okay then, with this new information Officer Lead I would like you to plot a new course with the assistance of Randalari."

The captain then came over the intercom once more and said, "With new and useful insight from one of our new crew members we are now leaving the planet of Celeriac and we will simply remain at the exterior of its atmosphere until we have a new course plotted. That is all Bridge out."

After completing his transmission Captain Owens looked at First Officer Lead and said, "I think I am going to go get some coffee." Immediately following this comment, he exited the bridge and began to make his was to the mess facility. Once Captain Owens arrived at the mess facility, he grabbed a cup of coffee and sat by one of the exterior windows and looked at the stars in amazement. While sitting there one of the mess facility operators began to clean a table across from the captain. Seeing this individual, the captain looked at the young female and said, "Sit down with me for a second Ma'am. The young female sat down across from the captain hesitantly and said, "Yes sir how can I be of assistance." The captain then said, "Your company is all I ask at the moment. With that, I ask you what do you think of our mission so far?"

The young female looked at the captain and said, "I never thought that I would see other intelligent lifeforms, let alone become friends with them. I also never dreamed I would travel to other galaxies."

Captain Owens then responded, "I know how you feel. Many years ago, I didn't think I would ever Captain a ship again. However, here I am. Although it is not with some regret. I did not know that we would be lost in the endlessness of space when we first entered the black hole that led us here."

The young female then responded, "No one blames you for us being here. We are thankful that you are our Captain. I think that you have handled our situation in an amazing manner. All of us knew that we might not be able to return to our home. However, if it will better mankind then it has been worth it." Captain Owens acknowledged what the girl had said, thanked her for her time, and then stood up to make his way back to the bridge.

While walking down one of the main corridors Captain Owens decided he was going to once again visit what had come to be known as the Relic Room. Once at the Relic Room Captain Owens discovered one of the new crew members just standing in the room staring at one of the statues that they had collected. Seeing this Captain Owens approached the individual. Once by his side he said, "Beautiful, aren't they? It is amazing how someone could just abandon something of such beauty."

The individual now paying attention to the captain then said, "What do you mean abandon?"

The captain simply responded, "The planet that we found them on was completely empty. However, it had sculptures of great beauty. We took these few in hopes that we eventually would be able to find answers as to what happened to the people there."

The individual then said, "These sculptures are not from this galaxy. I have been to every planet within this solar system and some from the next. These sculptures came from somewhere else. It is very possible that the planet itself passed through the dark hole, much like you did, and ended up here."

Captain Owens then said, "What do you mean passed through the dark hole?"

The individual then responded, "Well sometimes when we are running low on certain resources we pass through the dark hole at the edge of our galaxy and go to the next one to collect what we need. Once we are done, we come back here. Sometimes however, if something is close enough to the dark hole it will be pulled into it."

Captain Owens now curious then said, "How were you able to return to your original location once you passed through the black hole?"

The individual then said, "Well we found that the key was to not actually fly into the empty-space or as you call them black holes but to let its gravitational pull, pull you in. Ships that we had fly into the dark hole never returned. However, those that let the dark hole pull them in have been able to return without issues."

Hearing this Captain Owens looked at the individual and said, "I need you to come with me to the bridge immediately." Somewhat startled by the captain's response the new crew member complied. The two men then made their way to the bridge quickly. Once on the bridge Captain Owens looked at First Officer Lead and said, "He has told me how we can pass through a black hole and then return to the original spot that we entered." First Officer Lead now looking at the man asked him to explain the process. In which he did. After explaining it, Randalari shook his head and acknowledged. First Officer Lead then began to question the two individuals. His first question was could they pass back through previous black holes and end up at the location they started at.

Randalari at this point chimed in and said, "Sir if you flew into what you call a black hole then the answer is no. Flying into the black hole for some reason changes or alters your overall path. Where that path leads there is no way to know. However, as he stated before if you simply let the black hole pull you in, and do the same thing when you are exiting a galaxy then you will go back to your original location."

After hearing this the captain and First Officer Lead knew that they needed to try this technique to see if it actually worked. With that in mind Captain Owens looked at Randalari and said, "I want you to plot a course for the black hole or the point of entry we used when entering this galaxy." Randalari did so without hesitation.

As soon as the course was plotted, he looked at the captain and said, "Sir, in order to return to the galaxy that you originally came from you will have to find a new black hole that leads you there."

The captain looked at Randalari and said, "I understand that son, but you have just given us new hope. If this process works with our ship as well, at least we will be able to return to galaxies that we explore in the future to include this one, and we will know where each black hole leads." After finishing with this statement Randalari simply said that he understood and then looked at the captain and told him that the journey to the black hole would take approximately six days.

The next six days proved to be the longest of any of the crew member's lives that knew what Randalari and his companion had said. However, Eclipse 8 continued to approach their destination at a constant speed. Each leader among Eclipse 8 remaining hopeful but silent. As no one wanted to get other personnel's hopes up; however, all prayed that this new information was the key to being able to return to their loved ones once the proper black hole was found.

On the sixth day Eclipse 8 sat in front of the black hole they had been waiting to reach. As they sat a short distance from the black hole Captain Owens looked at First Officer Lead and said, "First Officer Lead, get us to a point that it feels as if the ship is being pulled and then have the engine room kill the engines." First Officer Lead shook his head and then started to creep the ship forward. Right before

Eclipse 8 entered the point of no return, Captain Owens came over the intercom and said, "Brace yourself everyone and prepare to enter the abyss once again." He immediately hung up this time though and did not follow with another comment.

Now in the gravitational pull of the black hole First Officer Lead called the engine room and told them to shut down the engines. Confused at this point the engine room complied. Moments later the ship was pulled into the black hole just as the new members said it would be. About five minutes passed before the ship surfaced on the other side. Once there, Captain Owens immediately began to give commands.

As soon as Eclipse 8 was clear of the black hole Captain Owens called the engine room and said, "Fire the engines back up." Following this transmission, he looked at First Officer Lead and said, "Full ahead until we are clear of the black hole's gravitational pull. Once we are clear I want you to chart the stars. That way if we are able to pass back through to the same galaxy, we can ensure this is where we end up a second time."

First Officer Lead complied. Upon completion he looked at Captain Owens and said, "Sir we have completed with charting the new galaxy. However, are you sure you want to—"

Before he could even finish his statement Captain Owens looked at him and said, "First Officer Lead, turn the ship around and prepare once again to enter the black hole." First Officer Lead looked at the captain in shock and immediately turned the ship around.

Now nearing the black hole, a second time, Captain Owens called the engine room and again told them to shut down the engines. Once they were shut down First Officer Lead looked at Captain Owens and said, "Sir are you going to warn the rest of the ship?"

Captain Owens smiling now said, "No, I am not, it is better they do not know the madness that we are attempting right now." About that time, the ship was once again completely pulled into the black hole.

Now complete with their second trip though the black hole the ship sat motionless awaiting new orders. Knowing this Captain Owens immediately gave the command to start the engines and move the ship forward. Once the ship was a safe distance away from the black hole Captain Owens looked at First Officer Lead and said, "I want you to chart the galaxy and run it against already existing maps." First Officer Lead immediately began to chart the stars; however, about halfway through charting them a map automatically pulled up on the screen and showed 100% likeness. With a sigh of relief, the two men looked at each other and the captain said, "We have done it, Lead!" After saying this the captain grabbed the intercom and said, "I am sorry I did not tell you that we were entering a black hole a second time and I am also sorry for the mystery during our current travels. However, with the help of our new crew members we were able to pass through a black hole this time and return to our point of origin. This does not mean that we have found a way back to our galaxy. However, it does guarantee that we can now travel from galaxy to galaxy and return to any one galaxy at any point in time. This also allows us to know where each black hole leads. Which in turn, will help to eliminate many of them and better our chances of returning home."

Immediately following the transmission, you could hear the cheers all the way through the ship. After the cheers died down a little the captain then came back over the intercom and said, "Now unfortunately to ensure that this technique is flawless and will work every time we must once again pass back through the black hole. If when the stars are charted, the new chart matches the old one, then this technique will be verified. We will then continue on through that galaxy and continue our mission, in hopes that the black hole in the next galaxy leads us home. So without further hesitation, I ask everyone to brace their selves one last time."

Following this transmission Eclipse 8 once again turned around and approached the black hole. As before, once they were in the gravitational pull of the black hole, they cut the engines and let gravity take its toll. Moments later they arrived at the other side of the black hole. This time when they were clear of the hole though Captain Owens showed no hesitation, he called the engine room and said, "Fire the engines up and I want thrusters full ahead." After his transmission he looked at First Officer Lead and said, "Chart the stars to confirm." Once again First Officer Lead began to chart the stars, and much like before the chart pulled up a 100% match.

Chapter 23
The Black Planet,
Man's New Hope?

Now having a new sense of accomplishment all members of Eclipse 8 conducted their duties in a manner that had not been seen since the ship initially left Deep Space Command. All knew that they were far from being home and still had a mission to conduct, but had a newfound hope. That being said, First Officer Lead and Randalari continued to run scans of the planets within the new solar system. Even though Randalari and his people had been here several times before they had not conducted missions on each planet or looked for resources that would prove useful for Eclipse 8 or mankind.

First Officer Lead and Randalari ran scans for several days and yielded no results. However, during one of the scans the two men noticed something odd about one of the planets. When running scans of the planets only one proved to not have a protective atmosphere. However, the same planet looked to be hollow. Both men continuously overlooked the planet at first thinking that it was a dead planet. However, for some reason the two kept coming back to it when their results kept coming back negative for resources throughout the galaxy. After about a week of this Captain Owens began to worry. Knowing that they had to find something that could prove to be useful or move on he pulled the two men off to the side. Captain Owens looking at the two men with concern then said, "It has been a week and we have yet to generate any results. If there is nothing in this solar system that can prove to be valuable that is fine. However, if that is the case, I need to know now so that we can plot a course to the next black hole in hopes that it can produce something." After saying this, Randalari looked at First Officer Lead and the two men mumbled under their breath. After about a minute of this Captain Owens looked at the two and said,

"Is there something that you would like to share with me gentlemen?" First Officer Lead then looked at him and said, "Sir there is nothing here of value. However, there is a planet that Randalari has not been too. It is also the only planet that has sent back odd scans."

Captain Owens then replied, "Odd, how?" First Officer Lead then told him of the findings that they had continuously gotten from the planet.

Captain Owens now baffled looked at First Officer Lead and said, "Well I guess this galaxy will not be a complete waste. Make a course for the planet in hopes that it holds a hidden treasure. If it is hollow is there an entrance?"

First Officer Lead then replied, "There is no entrance that we can see. By looking at the planet I feel our only hope of reaching the center is to drill through the surface in hopes that it doesn't affect the integrity of the planet."

Captain Owens then said, "Make it happen Lead! What do we have to lose a planet that holds no value to us?"

After his conversation with the captain, First Officer Lead plotted the new course in the ships navigational system. Once the ship began to follow the course First Officer Lead looked at Randalari and said, "The bridge is yours. I need to go talk to the engineers and Gauge to see if we even have anything that can penetrate the surface of the planet." Randalari responded with roger sir and First Officer Lead left the bridge.

After walking through most of the ship First Officer Lead had finally reached the weapons and defense level. Gauge immediately walked over to greet First Officer Lead as soon as he entered the level. After shaking his hand, he looked at First Officer Lead and said, "What can I do for you sir?"

Lead immediately responded, "I need a weapon or drill that can penetrate though 17 feet of pure rock like substance."

Gauge then asked, "What type of rock like substance? Is it layered? Is it solid? Because those are all factors that will make a difference?"

Lead then replied with, "Well that is just it! We won't know until we are on the planet's surface."

Gauge now scratching his head said, "I will come up with something sir. I guess plan for the best and expect the worst. I will simply fit the weapon with different settings so that it can be turned up or turned down based off of what you are trying to blast through."

Thinking the conversation was over Gauge began to walk away, then First Officer Lead said, "Oh yeah it is going to need to be affixed to the Voyager." Gauge then walked away muttering under his breath.

The only thing First Officer Lead could make out is when he said, "Fine I will make it look like a gypsy wagon." Hearing this First Officer Lead began to laugh and made his way back to the bridge.

Upon reaching the bridge Captain Owens had already returned. Captain Owens simply looked at Lead and said, "Hopefully you have solved some issues!"

First Officer lead shook his head and said, "Roger sir all the issues we know of at this point in time. However, the weapon that Gauge is preparing may or may not do the trick. He said that there are variables that can come into play, such as the type of rock that we have to go through."

Captain Owens just laughed and said, "There always is!"

Days later Gauge called up to the bridge and informed the captain that the weapon system was ready and had been affixed to the Voyager. Hearing this news Captain Owens looked at Randalari and asked him how close they were to reaching their destination. Randalari then told the captain that they were three days from the planet. While standing on the bridge Captain Owens started to wonder what the black planet had in store for them, as each planet that they had explored had produced unexpected results.

Now at the planet Captain Owens told First Officer Lead that he would be in charge of the exploration party. Hearing this he made his way to the Voyager with the rest of the crew. Once aboard the Voyager all crew fastened in and made their way to the surface or what they thought to be the surface of the planet. Upon touching down with the

Voyager scans showed that the surface was 20 not 17 feet of solid rock. Upon finding this out First Officer Lead called Captain Owens and asked him to have Gauge determine a setting that would accomplish their mission. Captain Owens did so, however, the response he got in return was not one that was expected. When Captain Owens called Gauge and informed him of the situation, Gauge said, "They told me 17 feet so that is what the machine was built for. It may or may not go through 20 feet. Tell them to set it on high frequency sir. One of two things will happen. The laser will blow up or they will crack through the surface." Hearing this raised some concern for the captain. After hearing this, he asked Gauge what the chances were of the laser blowing up.

Gauge immediately responded with, "Well, do you like to gamble sir? Because their chances are fifty fifty or about the same as hitting a seven when shooting craps."

Captain Owens after hearing this called First Officer Lead back and told him what Gauge had said. He then told First Officer Lead to return to the ship and they would re-evaluate the situation. However, First Officer Lead replied, "Sir I think I will take my chances. I am feeling kind of lucky today, and I have always been a gambler." Before anything else could be said First Officer Lead turned off the communication system on the Voyager. He then told the laser operator to begin operations. The laser operator did so for almost two hours when a loud cracking noise could be heard. Upon hearing this noise, the whole crew could feel the surface below the ship begin to move.

Thinking that the laser had destroyed the integrity of the planet First Officer Lead immediately gave the order to return Eclipse 8. Upon their arrival at Eclipse 8 First Officer Lead was greeted by a very angry Captain. Captain Owens furious at this point told the crew to return to their perspective levels and then began to yell at Lead furiously. However, midway through the scolding Randalari called down to the docking bay and said, "Captain Owens, I need you up here now. I think there is something that you need to see."

The two men hearing this frantically made their way back to the bridge. Randalari immediately greeted the two men and said, "What we thought was a hollow planet is not hollow at all. The hard substance that you began to drill through is some sort of casing that has covered the planet's atmosphere. When running scans while you were returning to the ship it showed that this planet is almost a perfect match to that of a young planet earth." Shocked by this both men made their way to the bridge windows. However, the planet was still completely encased in the black substance. Seeing this both men started brainstorming on how they could remove the hard casing. Thinking back on the laser, the captain then ran to the intercom and called Gauge to the bridge. Upon his arrival Captain Owens looked at him and asked, "The laser that you fitted the Voyager with, how similar is it to Eclipse 8's lasers?"

Gauge looking at the two men puzzled replied, "It is the same idea; however, the ships lasers are more concentrated and definitely more powerful."

Captain Owens then said, "If you were to turn the power on the lasers all the way down and we were to graze the surface of the planet would it have the same affect?"

Gauge now thinking said, "Yes sir it should; however, if you were directly to hit the planet's surface it might force a hole all the way through the planet." After hearing this Captain Owens told Gauge to go back to the lasers and turn them down as far as he could.

After Gauge called back up to the bridge telling them that the task was complete Captain Owens gave the command to reposition the ship so that the laser would barely touch the surface of the planet. Now in position Captain Owens looked at First Officer Lead and said, "Let's hope that this works. If not, this was all for nothing." Seconds later Captain Owens gave the command to fire a single shot from the ship's lasers. Barely glancing the planet. However, nothing happened with the first shot. Determined Captain Owens gave the command to fire once again. However, again nothing happened. Immediately after the second shot he gave the command to fire again. However, this time black pieces flew from several different places along the planet's surface. Seconds later all of the black substance that had once covered the planet was gone. Reveling a planet that looked exactly like the earth many of them had once known.

Now seeing this beautiful new planet Captain Owens gave First Officer Lead the command to report back to the Voyager and conduct testing on the planet's surface. Once all personnel were back aboard the voyager the ship quickly exited Eclipse 8 and made its way to the true surface of the planet. Once the Voyager touched down on the surface, the crew ran their normal scans. Upon receiving feedback from these scans, it was found that the soil, air, and atmosphere were the exact same as Earth.

Now having all of the results from the scans the crew exited the voyager and began taking samples of the resources that surrounded them. About three hours into the encounter on the planet without notice First Officer Lead removed his helmet. Immediately upon removing his helmet he began to cough and everyone feared the worst. However, seconds later he regained his composure. Upon regaining his composure, he took a deep breath and said, "This is the cleanest air I think that I have ever breathed." At that moment all personnel removed their helmets. Hours passed as the crew conducted operations moving about frantically to collect all of the samples that they could. Upon finishing grabbing samples, the Voyager made its way back to Eclipse 8 for the samples to have secondary tests run on them. It seemed at this moment that the mission had been a success and that mankind would get a second chance at survival. That is if they could find their way home.

Chapter 24
A Short Lived Victory

Even though operations had been concluded and the mission seemed to be a success, everyone aboard Eclipse 8 knew that their time on the black planet was far from over. If the tests conducted on the samples proved to be of significance more samples would need to be taken to verify findings. Eclipse 8 would not be able to move from its current position until every piece of useful knowledge and information possible could be gathered from the planet. To include the length of days and nights on the planet. The crew would also need to find out if now that the hard outer casing on the planet had been removed if vegetation would begin to grow. As if the climate on the planet did not allow plant life to grow it would in turn be useless to them.

Days passed and the crew continued to monitor the planet. Researchers consistently traveled on the Voyager to the surface of the planet to gather samples and raw materials that did exist. After about three weeks of conducting tests on samples, while on the planet's surface, Alazana noticed what looked to be a spec of green coming out of the ground. Curious Alazana continued to get closer to the object until he could tell that the green was in fact a sprout from a plant.

What type of plant remained unknown, but it was a form of life nonetheless.

To many individuals this was all the proof that was needed. However, Mr. Red the specialist in this area said that they would need to continue to monitor the surface of the planet in hopes that more plant life would come to exist. He stated that his major concern was although they had found a sprout, weather on the planet's surface may not be consistent enough to sustain that life.

In turn, what was supposed to be a one-day encounter turned into a month-long process. At the one-month mark there was so much green on the planet that it could be seen from Eclipse 8. It was at this point that Mr. Red concluded that plant life could be sustained on the black planet. Which in turn meant that human life could be sustained on the planet.

Now having all of the information that they needed Captain Owens told the crew that they would remain in place for 48 more hours until all findings from the planet were consolidated in an orderly manner, so that they could be presented to the L.I.G.H.T committee if the crew was able to return home. This would also prevent the crew from having to return back to this location due to any paperwork being lost or inconclusive data or results. As L.I.G.H.T. would not fund another voyage to this location if the crew was not able to provide them with all of the necessary information.

Mid-way through the first night while many members of the crew slept one of the individuals on the bridge noticed what seemed to be another ship on their radar. However, unlike before when the ship came up on the radar, Eclipse 8 began to receive what sounded to be L.I.G.H.T transmissions. Hearing these broken transmissions, the individual alerted the captain. The captain upon this news immediately sprung out of his bed and made his way to the bridge. Once on the bridge, he told the individual manning the ships communication system to turn the transmission up. All members of the bridge sat for several minutes trying to decipher what the transmission was saying. However, none were able to make it out, as it was interrupted with too much white noise. One thing members of the crew did agree on though was that they heard the transmission mention L.I.G.H.T.

With that in mind Captain Owens stated, "Until we can be certain what is being said in the transmission we will remain in our current location. If the ship continues to move this way and no communication is established and we cannot clearing identify them as part of L.I.G.H.T. we will fire a warning shot at them when they are within weapon range." All personnel simply acknowledged the captain's orders.

Individuals continued to watch the ship approach their location until early in the morning. Around 0700 hours the ship that had been continuously moving toward them halted just short of the ships weapon range. Seeing this First Officer Lead now manning the bridge called Captain Owens to his location. Once at First Officer Leads location, Captain Owens asked him what was going on. First Officer Lead simply responded, "Sir the ship has stopped."

Captain Owens replied, "Why have you called me up here for that? Have we been able to establish a clear line of communication, or been able to identify any markings on the ship?"

Lead then said, "No on all counts, sir. However, the reason that I called you up here is that I feel there is room for concern. The ship that approached us has stopped just short of our weapons capability and has not moved for several hours now." Hearing this Captain Owens also felt that there was a reason to be concerned.

He then looked at First Officer Lead and said, "Get everyone to their battle stations. Once we have received a status from all levels have Gauge bring up the ships defensive shield and ready the weapon systems."

About twenty minutes after giving this command all personnel were at their proper positions and the ship had been readied for battle if the situation presented itself. Upon these tasks being completed First Officer Lead looked at Captain Owens and said, "Sir, we are awaiting your next order." Captain Owens sat hesitantly for a moment before responding.

He then said, "Move the ship forward slowly." As soon as the ship began to move a green laser was fired at Eclipse 8. Captain Owens now knew that this other ship was not friendly. Seeing this Captain Owens ordered a shot be returned at the enemy ship. Once the shot was fired the enemy ship remained still for an extended period. Until all at once the ship started to move forward and began to fire a constant beam at Eclipse 8. Captain Owens at this point ordered evasive maneuvers to be conducted. After giving this command Eclipse 8 moved swiftly away from the incoming fire. However, when it did it revealed a second ship.

Upon seeing the second ship Captain Owens knew that they would need to evade the two enemy ships as they would not stand a chance in a two on one battle. In turn, he ordered the ships cloaking device be engaged and an emergency evacuation route taken. As soon as the command was given Eclipse 8 went invisible to the naked eye. However, it was still visible to the other ships that were pursuing them. As Eclipse 8 moved at the speed of light through space the other two ships continued to follow them firing shots at them at every opportune moment. After several minutes of this First Officer Lead looked at Captain Owens and said, "Sir, we are going to have to make a stand if we want any chance at survival." Knowing that he was right Captain Owens sat and thought about what actions could be taken that could possibly separate the two enemy ships from each other. After thinking for a few moments Captain Owens felt that their only chance was to enter a black hole with the ship's thrusters at full ahead. As he knew from previous experience that this would lead to the ships being separated. However, it would also lead to the crew losing the black planet and all of the knowledge and allies they had gained up to this point.

Not wanting to lose these things Captain Owens looked at First Officer Lead and asked, "Can you fly us by the black hole at a distance that would cause the other ship to be pulled in?"

First Officer Lead now quickly doing calculations responded, "The only way that would be able to be achieved is if they were right beside us and we turn in a manner that doesn't allow them to see the black hole until it is too late."

Captain Owens then said, "I know the chances of this working are slim. But go ahead and program a second navigational path that will bring us back to the black hole. If we fail to get the other ship to go in the black hole, we will enter it to keep from being destroyed. If this does work, we will stand and fight the remaining ship." First Officer Lead acknowledged Captain Owens and began programming courses into the computer.

When he was finished, he looked at the captain and said, "Sir we are ready for evasive maneuvers." Upon hearing this Captain Owens told the engine room to increase thrusters to maximum power.

Eclipse 8 and the enemy ship were now traveling so fast they almost looked to be two streaks of light passing through the night sky. As they approached the black hole First Officer Lead sat screaming distances to the captain. However, the captain sat fearless of what lay ahead. It wasn't until Eclipse 8 was less than 1000 meters from the black hole that Captain Owens gave the command to begin banking maneuvers. As the ship slowly turned the enemy ship followed almost beside them now. It was at that time the enemy ship realized that the black hole was there and tried to quickly bank the opposite way to avoid the anomaly. However, it was too late. The ship had hit the black hole in just a manner that allowed it to be grabbed in the black hole's gravitational pull.

Now with only one ship left to face Eclipse 8 stood more of a chance of survival. Knowing this Captain Owens looked at First Officer Lead and told him to do whatever he could to come up behind or beside the other ship. However, the two ships continued to chase each other through space neither gaining ground on the other. Several minutes after the chase began Alazana and Randalari both looked at Captain Owens and stated that they would not be able to out maneuver the opposing ship that if they stood a chance it would have to be in terms of weapon capabilities. Fearful that this moment would come, Captain Owens ordered First Officer Lead to place them in a defensive position.

Now in a defensive position the enemy ship once again approached them firing several shots at Eclipse 8 all hitting with precision. Suffering blow after blow Captain Owens gave the command to return fire. The two ships sat firing at each other for several minutes before either ship showed to incur any damage. However, after about ten minutes' lights started to illuminate on Eclipse 8's control panel showing that one of the lower-level corridors had been breached. Seeing this Captain Owens began to fear for the worst. However, in that moment he did not lose hope. Instead, he ordered for the breached section of the ship to be sealed. After giving this command he called Gauge over the intercom and said, "Son I am going to need you to give me a little more than that. Right now, we are doing no damage."

Gauge quickly responded, "Sir if we cut the engines momentarily, I can focus all of the energy to the lasers. However, we need to absorb the blast from one of their lasers moments before you cut the engines. That will give us enough power we should be able to destroy the other ship. Everything has to be timed perfectly though."

Captain Owens at this point was willing to give anything a shot. Now having this information from Gauge, Captain Owens looked at First Officer Lead and said, "I need you to fire at them in a manner that will cause them to fire defensively. When they are about to fire back let me know. Keep the intercom system open so at that moment I can reach both Sun Tu and Gauge." First Officer Lead simply acknowledge. Right about that time First Officer Lead began firing a series of shots at the other ship.

About three minutes into this series of shots First Officer Lead looked at Captain Owens and said, "Prepare for counter fire." It was at that moment that Captain Owens told Sun Tu to cut the engines. When Gauge heard this, he redirected all of the energy of the ship to the lasers. Moments after this energy was redirected the ship began to shake and then a shot was fired like none that had ever been seen before. The blast that had been fired by Eclipse 8 had completely destroyed the enemy ship. The only thing that had remained of the enemy ship was fragments and pieces of the ship that were floating around in space.

At that moment, everyone felt relief. However, the battle had taken a toll on Eclipse 8. The ship now had 22 members whose life had been taken due to the battle and damage that would take at least a month to repair before the ship would be mobile once again.

Chapter 25
Damages Repaired and a Mission Continued

Even though the battle was over there was no rejoicing this time. Individuals did not clap and yell in happiness. Instead, everyone walked around in a state of remorse. Everyone feeling a slight depression due to the members of the crew that had been lost. In all 22 crewmembers had their life taken throughout the conflict, and another 15 had been injured. Most of these individuals were on the lower levels when the haul of the ship had been breached. Some of those individuals were killed by the blast itself and others by the pressure of space rushing into the ship. Those that didn't fall into the two categories were simply injured by collateral damage on other levels. However, those that remained were happy that they were still alive.

After the conflict was over and damages were assessed, Captain Owens and First Officer Lead made their way around the ship to assess not only the damages the ship sustained, but also the mental status of personnel that had not been injured or killed in the engagement. After talking with many members of the crew it was apparent that many of them were fearful of what the future may hold. They felt that anything positive that they accomplished was overshadowed by the negatives that usually followed.

Captain Owens however did not say anything to lift spirits while he talked to individuals. Instead, he felt that it would be better to address everyone as a collective group. Now walking toward the area that sustained a majority of the damage Captain Owens noticed little known maintenance operator David Nash. A man that was responsible for most operations that kept day to day life running aboard Eclipse 8. Although many never thanked David, Captain Owens did every time he encountered him. As he knew the role that the man filled and the problems that he overcame regardless of the circumstances.

Upon greeting David, Captain Owens said, "Mr. Nash what do you think about all of this?"

David stood for a minute before answering and then said, "Sir sometimes bad things happen to good people. But in those times, we must be resilient. We must show that we are able to bounce back and overcome adversity. If we do not make an attempt to overcome obstacles and situations that we are faced with we will most definitely fail. However, if we do try to overcome these obstacles we increase or odds of becoming victorious. That is not only what separates winning from losing, but also life from death in many cases. It is tragic that we have lost so many members of the crew. However, we have also gained many people along the way. I am not saying that we should not mourn our losses, but the crew should be reminded of their victories and accomplishments. I feel at this moment if the crewmembers of Eclipse 8 are not positively stimulated then many of them will shut down and feel that our mission has been a failure and any hope of returning home is a lost cause."

Surprised by this answer Captain Owens looked at the man in shock and said, "I completely understand what you have said David and I will most definitely take your advice. You are wise beyond your year's sir. On another note, how bad do you think the damages are, and how long do you think they will take to fix." Mr. Nash now looking through a small window of the sealed off corridor replied, "Well that depends on you and others among the ship sir. It doesn't really matter what I think. I am simply one man. I can make a slight difference. However, if everyone works together, we can progress in leaps and bounds and have the damages repaired in around two to three weeks." Captain Owens simply looked at Mr. Nash as this point nodded his head and replied, "Understood sir and I thank you for what you have done already."

Upon finishing his statement Captain Owens and First Officer Lead made their way back toward the bridge. However, when they were passing through the corridor where they lived, Captain Owens looked at First Officer Lead and said, "I think I will retire for a little bit. If you don't mind, could you take control of the bridge until my return." First Officer Lead then acknowledged the captain and returned to the bridge. While the captain turned down another long corridor and retired to his cabin.

Once inside his cabin Captain Owens sat down at his desk and simply stared out his window into the vastness of space. While sitting there, Captain Owens became lost in thought as he had no idea at this point what to say to the crew. As even he had not encountered a situation such as this throughout his career. After several hours, Captain Owens knew it was time to address the crew and do whatever he could to lift spirits, and if spirits could not be lifted at least motivate the crew to at least try to continue on.

Captain Owens after thinking about the situation long and hard came to the conclusion that the best motivation he could give the crew at this point was the truth. With this in mind Captain Owens made his way back up to the bridge. Once on the bridge he immediately came over the intercom system and said, "I know right now many of you are feeling down. Many of you are even ready to give up. I would actually be lying to you if I said that I have not thought about it once or twice. However, accepting failure will get us nowhere. If we simply lay down and accept defeat, we are doing ourselves an injustice. We are doing those who sacrificed their life and mankind an injustice. We were all selected for this mission because we were and are the best in our fields. We were chosen for this mission because no one else had the testicular fortitude to step forward. I ask you now at our lowest point, that you step forward and be the leaders that I know you can be. I expect you to rise above the devastation that we have just experienced and find ways to ensure that the same thing does not happen again. I expect you to continue on for not only yourself, but those that you have left behind and those that we have lost. Ask yourself if we do not step forward, who will, and if we do not take action now, when will we. If you ever want to see your loved ones again, if you want to return to L.I.G.H.T. victorious and as saviors to mankind and the human race remind yourself of these things. If we all work together and continue to pursue a common goal, then we will most definitely succeed. As failure is only experienced most often when individuals stop pursuing their goals. So now in this most critical time, I ask you to search your soul and decide what action you will take. If you want to accept failure, we will accept failure as a whole and sit here lifeless in space until we are overrun by enemies or die from lack of resources. However, if you want to be successful, we will work together as a whole to repair the ship and continue on with our mission. In turn, increasing our chances of survival and once again returning home." After he completed with his speech Captain Owens turned off the intercom and remained in his seat. At which point First Officer Lead simply looked at him and nodded his head in approval.

The first 24 hours after the captain's speech there still seemed to be no change in overall demeanor throughout the ship. However, two days afterwards something changed. It almost seemed as if a positive mindset was spreading throughout the ship like a virus. As the captain walked to the mess hall the way he did every morning he noticed that there were several people moving about the corridors. Once at the mess hall he looked at one of the workers and asked them what was going on and what all of the commotion was about. The worker simply replied, "Last night each level leader had a meeting with their perspective crews. During the meeting they simply took your advice sir. I think your advice mixed with not wanting to die did the trick." The worker then laughed and handed the captain a plate and walked away.

After finishing his breakfast, the captain began to walk around the ship. While walking around the captain noticed that many of the areas that sustained collateral damage had been fixed, and the area that took the most of the blast was being repaired as well. Seeing this the captain once again had a renewed smile on his face and made his way to the bridge to get an overall status of operations.

Upon arriving to on the Bridge Captain Owens noticed that Randalari, Alazana, and First Officer Lead had several navigational charts up in front of them. Seeing this the captain's interest was sparked, so he moved to their location. Now standing beside First Officer Lead the captain asked, "What are you guys doing? It will be weeks before we can move."

First Officer Lead then said, "But when the ship is ready, we will be ready. Randalari and Alazana through research think they have found a way to get us to a parallel galaxy to our own. We hope if we can accomplish this, we will be able to establish communication once again with L.I.G.H.T command. It is a long shot sir, but if it works it will be well worth it." Hearing this the captain now had a grin that ran from ear to ear. Something that the crew had not seen in quiet some time.

With all of this information the captain felt it was best not to make a scene or inform anyone of his thoughts. He felt that a disturbance might hinder this new found motivation or give false hope. Instead, he sat down in his captain's chair and enjoyed the day.

The captain continued with this action for two more weeks until the ship was finally completed. Upon completion of repairs the captain knew the start-up procedure of the ship could make or break everyone's confidence. However, it was a process that could not be avoided. It was now or never. Knowing this the captain came over the intercom and said, "All leaders and crewmembers, at this time man your perspective areas of operation." Following this the captain, one by one, gave each level the order to start up operating systems. After all levels had powered up the ship once again was operational.

Now at full operating power the captain looked at First Officer Lead and said, "What is our next destination?"

First Officer Lead then replied, "The black hole just past the black planet." Captain Owens acknowledged his request and the ship was placed on the most direct route and headed toward their new destination.

Chapter 26
Is the End in Sight?

Now at the black hole the crew was once again ready to head into the unknown. As they approached the entrance Captain Owens looked at First Officer Lead and said, "Let's hope Alazana and Randalari's calculations are correct." Immediately following the command was given to cut the engines. Slowly Eclipse 8 was pulled into the black hole as it had been so many times before. As they exited into the new galaxy, Captain Owens once again ordered the ship's engines to be started. As the engines pushed the very large ship forward, he then gave Randalari and First Officer Lead the command to start a new navigational chart.

As they did this something happened that was not expected though. While they were charting the stars a map pulled up and said 50% comparison. Confused the two men ran the scan again, and once again they received the same results. At this point the only thing that First Officer Lead could think is, how is this possible? As they had not been to the galaxy they were currently in. Confused by the results First Officer Lead then called Captain Owens to his position and told him what his findings were.

After several minutes of conversing, Captain Owens came to the conclusion that the galaxy that they were in must have almost been a twin to one of the galaxies that they had traveled through in the past. After coming to this conclusion, he then told First Officer Lead to conduct an analysis of the planets and find which ones proved the most promising in terms of exploration. Immediately following he then order Alazana to start trying to reach L.I.G.H.T. command.

Both men immediately went to work without question. Moments later First Officer Lead looked at the captain and said, 'I have a new course sir. However, if the computer is correct, we have already conducted an exploration there. If the computer is correct the planet that we are moving to is in fact the first planet that we explored when beginning this mission. That planet being A1." Captain Owens then responded with, "I don't care what the computer says Lead. It is very well possible that the computer was in some way damaged or an error occurred during repairs to the ship. However, to settle this matter we will conduct in depth scans of the planet once we arrive. If the planet proves to be A1 then we will reassess our situation." First Officer Lead then put the coordinates into the ship and they began on their new course.

Travel to the new planet would take around one month. However, time was something that the crew had plenty of. While conducting movement to the new planet Eclipse 8 kept a clear line of communication open and continued to broadcast a distress signal in hopes that L.I.G.H.T. command would pick the signal up. However, days turned into weeks and Eclipse 8 received no response.

Now only one week away from the planet that they were going to conduct research on, the soon to be crew of the Voyager prepped for their mission. Each individual tasked with going conducted extensive research on scans to ensure that they did not miss anything. However, as each member of the crew reviewed scans all felt that it was a place that they had been before.

Days later, Eclipse 8 had reached the planet. Once arriving Captain Owens again ordered scans to be conducted on the planet. Each time the same results were reached though. All results showed that the planet that they had arrived at was in fact A1. Unwilling to admit this Captain Owens still ordered the crew to man the Voyager and move to the planet's surface.

Upon traveling to the planet's surface, the crew slightly altered the coordinates so that they would land where they thought they previously had. They all felt that if they had in fact been there before this would allow them to see marks where the Voyager had landed last time. However, all personnel knew if this was A1, they would have to be cognizant of the mosquitos that they had encountered the first time. That being said, all members of the crew were ordered to remain in their full suit upon exiting.

The Voyager was now sitting on the planet's surface and the ramp was being lowered. All members of the crew knew that this was the moment of truth. Upon exiting First Officer Lead gave the command to spread out and look for remnants of their last exploration. About three minutes after exiting the Voyager one of the military personnel yelled to First Officer Lead, "Sir you are going to want to see this." Hearing this First Officer Lead quickly made his way to the man. In front of the individual was clear marks of where the Voyager had landed the first time. After seeing this First Officer Lead immediately gave all personnel the command to re-board the ship.

After all personnel were back aboard the Voyager First Officer Lead called the captain. Immediately the captain said, "What have you found?"

Lead immediately said, "Sir we found the area where we landed the first time that we were here."

Captain Owens now confused as well then said, "So we are in fact in a solar system where we have previously been. Conclude operations and return to the Eclipse."

Now back on-board Eclipse 8 all personnel on the bridge were in an uproar. They had not been in this situation before so none knew what to do. Trying to calm the situation down Captain Owens told everyone to be quiet. After the bridge was silent Captain Owens called First Officer Lead and all the Level Heads to the conference room for a conference.

After all personnel were present, Captain Owens began to speak, "First we will discuss the facts. According to our navigational charts and findings on the planet's surface this is the galaxy that we first entered on our voyage. This was also the last galaxy that we were able to communicate openly with L.I.G.H.T. command. However, since we have returned, we have not been able to raise L.I.G.H.T. command or the Deep Space Station. This could be due to damage we sustained during our previous encounter. Regardless I am open to suggestions at this point."

All members of the crew at this point quietly whispered to each other before Sun Tu finally responded, "If all of the facts point to us being here before, then we should be able to raise L.I.G.H.T. command or the Deep Space Station. I vote that we stay in place until we are able to figure out our communication issues."

As soon as Sun Tu finished his comment many of the other level heads began to shout until the entire room was in an uproar. When this happened Captain Owens hung his head for a brief second and then yelled, "I will have order in here. You are all professionals and this will be handled in a professional manner. If anyone else has an idea I am listening."

It was then that Gauge said, "I vote we go through the black hole in hopes that it takes us back to our original location. What is the worst that can happen? We end up somewhere else! That would be the story of our life at this point."

Captain Owens was now deep in thought thinking of the two men's proposals. After thinking about the matter for a few minutes he then responded, "I like both of your proposals." Now looking at the captain confused all personnel started to shout again.

Once again though Captain Owens silenced the room by saying, "If we cannot raise L.I.G.H.T. command or the Deep Space Station within the next 48 hours then we will enter the black hole in hopes that it takes us home. If we are able to reach L.I.G.H.T. command or the Deep Space Station, we will then take all commands from them." Happy with this decision all personnel simply nodded and agreed.

While everyone exited the conference room Captain Owens stood patiently by the door. It was obvious that he was waiting on someone, but no one knew who. Until he pulled both Sun Tu and Gauge off to the side. Once he had the two men, he looked at both and said, "I want you two to work together. First, I want you to find a way to increase the radio signal that we are transmitting Gauge. Sun Tu, I want you to build a device that can be flown into the black hole and one that can simply be attached to the ship and can be released into the black hole and pulled back to the ship. If we are indeed, able to reach L.I.G.H.T. or the Deep Space Station I do not want to go in blind this time. If communication is established this will let us know the manner in which we will have to enter the black hole."

Upon finishing the conversation, the two men left the captain's side and made their way back to their own level to begin working on the captain's request. Hours later, Gauge called the bridge and told them to switch the frequency that they were broadcasting on to 1987266.01 MHz's. Operators among the bridge did so willingly. Hours after this still no communication was able to be established. Bound and determined to establish communication Gauge once again called the bridge and had them change the frequency on which they were broadcasting. However, this still generated no results.

Now out of ideas Gauge called the captain and told him that was the best he could do in terms of communication. However, to his surprise the captain was not upset. Instead, the captain responded with, "You did your best son that is all that matters. I want you to go ahead and fit whatever craft Sun Tu has designed with the same technology. However, since no one will be manning the craft, you will have to make it to where the frequency can be changed remotely from Eclipse 8." Gauge then acknowledged the captain and made his way to Sun Tu's location.

Now just moments away from their cutoff time Sun Tu and Gauge had completed everything the commander had asked of them. Knowing that communication was not able to be established the captain then gave the order to move just outside of the black hole's gravitational pull. However, what came next was a surprise to everyone. Now barely outside of the black hole the command interface display started to flicker. Moments later Eclipse 8 started to receive a response to their distress signal. Seeing this Captain Owens immediately gave the order to hold their position. However, through the broken response no one could tell who was returning their call. Was it an enemy ship, or had they finally reached L.I.G.H.T. command or the Deep Space Station?

Chapter 27
Eclipse 8 Reaches Its Long
Awaited Destination

Hours had now passed since Eclipse 8 received the broken response to their distress call and still they were no closer to being able to understand the response. However, operators worked around the clock to clear up the transmission. Operators tried everything from lengthening and shorting the antenna that they were broadcasting from to adjusting the signal. About 29 hours into this process everyone's efforts were justified though. Just when operators were starting to run out of ideas and beginning to get frustrated the captain came over the intercom and said, "Everyone stop what you are doing right now!" They had done it.

After telling everyone to stop what they were doing the command interface screen flickered a couple of times and then it revealed President Hays. Everyone on the bridge immediately started screaming in rejoice. Captain Owens however asked them to all keep the noise down and began talking to President Hays. To start off the conversation Captain Owens said, "Sir, you are the best sight any of us have seen in a very long time. We had all but lost hope of seeing you again." However, before he could finish with his long-prepared speech President Hays cut him off in disbelief.

Before he could finish, President Hays had noticed Alazana and Randalari and said, "What or who on Earth are those people manning the bridge, Captain Owens?"

At that time Captain Owens said, "Sir, if you bring us home, I will tell you all about it." Following this statement Captain Owens informed President Hays that they were now back in the original galaxy that they had entered. He then went on to tell the President of his intentions with the shuttles. Surprised and confused by this President Hays told Captain Owens to continue with the plan that he had in place and he would inform L.I.G.H.T. command and the Deep Space Station. He did however ask the captain to wait to initiate any actions until everyone was aware of what was about to take place.

Hours later President Hays came back over the command display interface. Upon his return President Hays told the captain that they would be ready to hopefully retrieve the crafts.

Within the next couple of hours several working parts went into action. The first thing that happened was Sun Tu prepared the first craft for flight by sending it out of the docking bay doors. Once the craft was outside of Eclipse 8 Sun Tu slowly positioned it. He then called the captain and said, "Sir do you want the first craft to be jettisoned into the black hole, or do you want to simply let it be pulled in by the gravitational pull?"

Captain Owens hesitated for a moment and then responded, "I want you to jettison it into the black hole. That is how we initially came through. Hopefully, if it exits the same way we entered then it will be retrieved by L.I.G.H.T. command and the Deep Space Station." After making this comment Captain Owens then came back over the command interface display and told President Hays to prepare to receive the package. At the exact same time, he also gave Sun Tu the order to initiate the launch. Moments later, Sun Tu came over the intercom and said the package has been sent.

Minutes had turned into an hour and still nothing had been received by L.I.G.H.T. command or the Deep Space Station. Puzzled by this President Hays responded to Eclipse 8 and said, "You did send the shuttle through, correct?"

Captain Owens responded, "Yes sir the package was sent and should have been received some time ago. We have found that the longest time it should take to pass through a black hole regardless of the method you use should be no more than five minutes."

President Hays then responded to the captain by saying, "I will have all available operators conduct scans of the immediate area to ensure that it wasn't missed. However, if the scans do not reveal anything what will your next course of action be?" Captain Owens responded by telling the president if the shuttle could not be found that they would simply let the second shuttle be pulled into the black hole by its gravitational pull.

After conducting several scans L.I.G.H.T command and the Deep Space Station produced no results. Upon coming to this conclusion President Hays once again contacted Captain Owens and told him that they were unable to find the craft and to go ahead and send the next one. Captain Owens complied by calling Sun Tu and telling him to prepare the second shuttle.

Sun Tu immediately followed the captain's orders and positioned the second shuttle behind Eclipse 8 just outside of the black hole's gravitational pull once again. Once in position Sun Tu called the captain and said, "Sir, I am ready and awaiting your command." Upon hearing this, Captain Owens informed President Hays that the next shuttle was being sent. He then told Sun Tu to allow the shuttle to be pulled in. Once the craft was gone, he then informed President Hays that the second shuttle had been sent.

As before Eclipse 8 waited a very long time and heard nothing from President Hays. About 45 minutes after the shuttle had been sent President Hays came over the command interface display and once again said that the shuttle had not been retrieved. At this point Captain Owens was confused. The tactic that they were using had worked flawlessly in the past. Unwilling to accept this answer Captain Owens told President Hays that they would continue to hold position and that he wanted L.I.G.H.T command and the Deep Space Station to continue to look for the second craft.

Hours later President Hays came over the command interface display once again. However, there was a look of happiness on his face. Captain Owens could tell that they had achieved their goal. At this point, President Hays said, "I am happy to inform you that although it did take quite a bit longer than 5 minutes, we were just now able to retrieve the second package moments ago." Captain Owens was now almost in tears. After hearing this, he looked at President Hays and said, "Sir with your permission I would now like to return to the Deep Space Station for port."

President Hays replied by saying, "We are at your disposal, Captain." Once the conversation was complete the command interface once again went black.

Captain Owens then came over the intercom and said, "I know that we have been tested and tried. I know that we have gained and lost great crew members. However, it was not in vain. Just moments ago, the second craft that we sent through the black hole was able to be retrieved by L.I.G.H.T command and the Deep Space Station. We are going home!" After finishing with his message Captain Owens looked at first Officer Lead and said, "Officer Lead if you would, one last time into the darkness." At that time Eclipse 8 was pulled into the black hole.

About five minutes after this Eclipse 8 arrived on the opposite side of the black hole in a galaxy that was all too familiar, and within eye sight you could see the Deep Space Station. Upon seeing the Deep Space Station Captain Owens established communication once more with mission control and said, "With the permission of L.I.G.H.T. command and the Deep Space Station Eclipse 8 is requesting permission to conduct docking procedures."

Immediately following the Deep Space Station replied, "You are clear to dock at port 5, and welcome back Eclipse 8." The crew of Eclipse 8 had done it. Not only had they embarked on a mission that had never been attempted before, but they returned victorious. As they had not only forged new treaties and discovered new intelligent lifeforms, but they had also returned with knowledge of a new inhabitable planet that would allow mankind to continue on as it always had and a clear path to reach it.